Jessica Carnegie

The Tale of The Ebony Queen

A Novel

THE TALE OF THE EBONY QUEEN

Published in the United States by SheEO Publishing Company, Locust Grove, VA 22508

ISBN-13: 978-0692608999

ISBN-10: 0692608990

Editing, Cover and Interior Design: SheEO Publishing Company www.SheEOPublishing.com
Author and Cover Photo: Morris Berryman

For general information or other products and services,
contact Jessica Carnegie at www.TaleOfTheEbonyQueen.com

Printed in the United States of America

The Tale of the Ebony Queen

SheEO PUBLISHING COMPANY

Dedicated to my Ebony Princess
Laeyla ♡

Once I was a prisoner. I was captivated by fear, bound by pain, and beaten with doubt, born into royalty yet afraid to accept my birthright. I abdicated my throne. Then I was challenged to accept my destiny. That which had me bound gave me strength. Fear no longer controlled me and all doubt began to perish. By accepting my birthright, I now reign with power and authority. Take heed, for a new Queen has risen.

~Jessica Carnegie

Do you accept the challenge?

Table of Contents

Chapter 1

Last night I had a dream. It didn't feel like a dream though; it felt more like I was in my own movie, and I was the star.

I was a princess just like Cinderella. Everyone loved me and told me I was beautiful and smiled when they said it. Then I met my prince and just like in the movie, we lived happily ever after.

That's what happens when you find your prince...you live happily ever after.

Eight-year-old Cheyenne yawns as she gets comfortable in her bed. "I can't wait until my prince comes and makes me a queen," she says out loud.

"I can't wait until you shut up so I can go to sleep," her younger sister Patrice says as she turns and pulls the covers over her head, returning to sleep.

☙☙☙

"Cheyenne, wake up. Cheyenne, get up honey. You have to get ready for school tomorrow."

"Okay, Mommy," Cheyenne says quietly as she comes up from her slumber.

Cheyenne looks at the television, which reminds her that in a few days it will be *Dress as Your Favorite Character Day* at school. "Mommy, can I wear my princess dress this Friday? Did you see my note from Mrs. Johnson? She said we can dress up as Disney characters!"

"It didn't say Disney characters, but yes I looked at it, Cheyenne."

"Well can I—please?" Cheyenne begs her mother.

"We'll see if it's been cleaned. You're always wearing that dress young lady."

Felicia Hudson turns and smiles at her oldest, beautiful baby-girl as she puts on her glasses, and smiles at the memory of when she had her on a hot summer day as she was picking up groceries in their southern, inner city neighborhood. She had decided to walk to the store that day, because all her friends where she worked as a social worker told her: *Walk around and that baby will come out sooner than you know it.*

Cheyenne came almost two weeks late, but Felicia didn't want to be induced; she insisted on having a natural delivery. No medicine for her.

"That medicine stuff will kill you," she would say. "My mom had all seven kids naturally, and I will have mine just the same," she told all her girlfriends at work.

When she stepped onto the gravel walkway that led back to her neighborhood from the store, she felt water in between her legs. She panicked, dropped her groceries, and walked...well, wobbled home as fast as she could, screaming, "Stanley! Stanley! She's coming. Get the car ready. Hurry. Our baby is coming!"

Her husband came out the house with one slipper on and his shirt unbuttoned. Felicia recalls how his pants weren't pulled all the way up because he was using the bathroom when he heard her yelling.

Funny thing is, they never made it to the hospital. Cheyenne was determined to come into this world, and she was on her way. Felicia knew she was coming because she reached down and felt something soft from her cavity.

"Pull over to Ms. Diane's house and see if we can use her phone," Felicia demanded from the back seat, where she was reclining. "This baby is coming!"

"Felicia, we don't know that woman. We can make it to the hospital," Stanley said as he picked up some speed. But once he turned around and saw the sweat pouring down her face, he knew he had better stop at Ms. Diane's house whether he knew her or not. He turned the air conditioner on to help cool his wife down and thought to himself that he was going to mess this all up.

Pretty, little Cheyenne Catherine Hudson was born in the bathtub of Ms. Diane, who happened to be a midwife and Cheyenne was her eighteenth delivery. She was the greatest gift that happened to the Hudson household. Her parents couldn't get enough of her and the miracle of her entrance into the world was the talk of the town. Everyone said she was determined to be here because she couldn't wait to make her mark in this world.

Cheyenne interrupts, "Mommy, are you going to look for my princess dress for Friday?"

"Yes, Cheyenne. Yes, I will."

Cheyenne runs to her mom and gives her a tight hug around her waist.

"You girls get off that couch and go to bed," Felicia tells her two children.

The girls get up and go to the room they share. Felicia turns the television off and ejects the *Cinderella* DVD out of the player and places it where Cheyenne will know where to find it.

Cheyenne is digging through all her clothes in the drawers, in the closet, and her dirty clothes hamper. She cannot find her princess dress. She starts to get furious and begins talking to herself out loud.

"Where is my dress? Where could it be? Dress, where are you?"

"Cheyenne be *quiet*," her little five-year-old sister barks from the bed.

"Where is my dress?" Cheyenne mumbles to herself, frantic that she won't find it to wear to school.

All she can think about is how pretty she's going to look. She can't wait to show all the other girls the long pink dress with silver beading that comes all the way down to her feet and moves when she walks and twirls. She wants them to see how pretty she is because they always laugh at her and call her goofy and weird. Cheyenne wants to prove to those girls that she can be beautiful. Once they see her in the dress, they will finally give her the validation she is looking for—at least this is what she believes.

"I wore it when Daddy took me to Brittany's birthday party. I think it's in Dad's car," Patrice says from under the covers.

"Patrice, don't wear my clothes. They are mine."

Patrice doesn't say anything; she is asleep again.

Cheyenne gets into bed making a mental note to search her daddy's car before he leaves to go to work in the morning. She looks at the clock that reads 8:13 p.m. and thinks: *He leaves in a few hours. I have to make sure I catch him before he leaves.*

Cheyenne's anxiety about her dress makes it hard to sleep. She finally dozes off and when she wakes up it's 6:00 a.m. She missed her dad by an hour. She cries herself back to sleep until her sister wakes her up to get ready for school.

"I don't want to get up. I had such a good dream," Cheyenne says as Patrice plays with her dolls on the floor.

Patrice comes and sits on Cheyenne's twin bed and says, "Tell me more about your dream."

"Oh yes, with Prince Charming," Cheyenne smiles.

"What's a prince charming?"

"He's a handsome boy who saves you at the ball. You dance with him and he marries you."

"Oh, I don't want no prince charming. I have Daddy. Boys are gross anyway," Patrice says, walking away uninterested.

"Prince Charming is better than Daddy, Tricie. He is what every girl wants, and he makes everything better." Cheyenne clears things up for her little sister. "Daddy doesn't do that."

"He does for me. Daddy is my Prince Charming."

Well, I want the real thing. I want to be a princess so my prince can find me. He will make things all better, and I bet those big head girls on the bus won't laugh at me then."

"What girls?" Patrice wants to know.

"Never mind," Cheyenne says and goes to brush her teeth and gazes at herself in the mirror. "I'm going to be a princess. Someone will love me. And I will be pretty because he will say so. I *will* be a princess."

A knock at the door breaks Cheyenne's daydream. "Mom said come to the kitchen for breakfast. Didn't you hear her?"

"I'm coming, Mom!" Cheyenne yells toward the kitchen, which was right down the hall from her room.

They live in an apartment so everything is pretty close and you can hear everything too. Cheyenne can't stand it. She always hears her mom talking loud to her dad, telling him what to do and how he needs to take her and Patrice more places and to stop spending all his time only with Patrice who was the youngest.

After the Hudsons had their two children, Cheyenne's mom always felt like her husband was a bad dad and that he never did anything with the family unless he was told. She also thought he favored Patrice because she had his mother's name. Stanley lost his mother from suicide just six months before Patrice was born. It was surprising to everyone, especially to her youngest and only son.

Stanley grew up around all girls. He was babied by all his sisters and had to learn how to cook, clean, wash dishes, do hair, and play dolls. Stanley grew up without his father, Will, who he's never met. Rumor has it, Will only came around to have sex with his mother and would stop coming around every time he found out she was pregnant. Sometimes his mother wouldn't even tell him she was pregnant because she knew he would disappear.

After the fourth pregnancy, Will just stopped coming. That hurt Stanley. He hated the man who created four bad kids with his mom and never came back to see his face, not even once, and it created a very tight bond between him and his mother and son. She knew Stanley was in a lot of pain and she felt guilty for Will's absence.

Since Stanley didn't have a father figure at home, he hung out with girls most of the time. He heard all the fighting and bickering and went through four different menstrual cycles each month. He was miserable but always knew he could go to his mom for comfort no matter who picked on him or whose nerves he was getting on at any given moment.

His mom called him *my mechanic* because young Stanley had a knack for fixing things around the house to help his mom out. Stanley couldn't talk about his mother without tears forming. He believes she wanted to kill herself many times, but her attempts failed. He remembers visiting her in a special hospital when he was a young boy where she would have to stay for weeks or even a few months at a time while he and his three older sisters went to their aunt's house.

Patrice looks just like her and Stanley does admit that is his angel.

Cheyenne says the extra attention to Patrice doesn't bother her, but Felicia thinks it does and often gets on Stanley about it

"You're not being fair to baby girl. You better spend more time with her," Felicia would demand from her husband speaking of Cheyenne.

"How many pieces of bacon do you want Cheyenne?" her mom asks.

"I don't want to eat, Mommy. I will get fatter."

"You're right. We don't need you to gain any more weight." She puts the bacon down and reaches for an apple to give Cheyenne.

"What time will Daddy be home? Did you find my dress?" Cheyenne anxiously asks her mother.

"Slow down girl, and you *are* going to eat this fruit before you go to school," her mom says. "He'll pick you up from school today. I asked him to take you to get ice cream then pick up Patrice from daycare."

Cheyenne didn't get the answer to her question. "Did you find my princess dress?"

"No. I couldn't find it. You'll have to wear something else."

Cheyenne bows her head down and looks at the food her mom has placed in front of her. She has no interest in eating. All she can think about was being a princess and praying to God that her dress was in her daddy's car.

Stanley is there on time to pick up Cheyenne, and she runs to the car to search for her dress. She spent her whole day at school thinking about her princess dress and how pretty she was going to look and how she would be the princess in school and everyone would admire her.

She doesn't have a lot of friends at school, just Shanice who's a little awkward like Cheyenne. No one cared to play with them. They both wear glasses, both are overweight, and pretty much stay to themselves most of the time, causing the other kids to pick on them at recess.

"What are you looking for?" Cheyenne's dad asks.

"Did you see my pink princess dress in here?"

"No."

Cheyenne is almost in tears. "I want my dress Daddy, so I can wear it to school tomorrow for character dress up day. I want to be a princess. Patrice said she wore it and left it in here. Did you see it?"

"No," Stanley replies. "Just wear something else. A Halloween costume will be fine, dear."

Cheyenne sits in the back seat looking out the window, unable to say a word. Her heart is broken. Tomorrow was supposed to be the day she shows up to the ball in her princess dress and have everyone admiring her. Her prince would show up and make everything better. She would be happy and no one would ever pick on her again. Tomorrow was the ball.

She sits silent, holding back her tears.

Stanley drives quietly thinking about what his wife has been saying about being there more for Cheyenne. He feels that maybe she's right.

"I'm going to stop at the store before we pick up Patrice, okay?"

"'Kay," Cheyenne says under her breath.

Stanley pulls into Toys R Us, looks at his daughter's sad face, and says, "Let's go get you that princess dress."

Cheyenne straightens up, looks at the big sign, and tries to hug her daddy before realizing her seat belt was still on. They share a giggle and he unfastens her seatbelt, walks over to her side of the door, and opens it for her.

"Madam," he says, gesturing with a sweeping motion for her to exit the car. Cheyenne links her arm into his and skips into the store.

Cheyenne smiles big and Stanley feels great.

Cheyenne set her alarm clock twenty minutes early so she could get herself together for her big day. She asked her mom to add pretty pink bows to her hair and comb it up real nice like on Easter Sunday. Cheyenne admires herself in the mirror and felt beautiful.

As soon as she gets on the school bus, the children laugh at her. They throw spit balls at her.

"Hey, Medusa! You sure look pretty today—*not!*" one chubby kid yells as the entire bus points and laughs at her.

Most of them are not even dressed, and she's all done up with hair bows, fancy shoes, and lip gloss.

As she walks down the aisle, everyone stares at her. "Are you going to a funeral, Cheyenne?" one girl asks then trips her as she walks passed.

"No, she's going to a pageant for most ugly princess," one boy says.

By this time Cheyenne is flat on her face humiliated. She gets up and walks to the back of the bus mortified. She cannot believe this is still happening to her after all she went through to be the princess she dreamed to be.

"Cheyenne, sit down please. You didn't ask to get out of your seat," Mrs. Libby says sternly. "We only have a few more minutes before class is dismissed."

Squirming in her seat, Cheyenne tells her teacher that she has to go to the bathroom and that she doesn't think she can hold it any longer—she knows it will take a long time to unbutton her dress costume from the back. She wants to take it off before she has to get back on the bus to go home, not wanting to go through that horror again.

Mrs. Libby asks Denise, her studious teacher's assistant, "Please take this child to the bathroom. And hurry back."

Cheyenne innocently grabs Denise's hand and they do a hurry-walk into Christian Faith Academy's little girls' room. The bathroom is the size of a small walk-in closet, with one sink and one stall. Cheyenne wanted to get in there first before all the kids in her classroom made a dash for the bathrooms when the bell rang.

Cheyenne is usually able to go into the bathroom by herself as a school staff member waits outside, but this time Denise wanted to come in with her. She explains she just wants to wash her hands.

While standing at the sink Denise asks, "How old is your sister?"

"Five," Cheyenne replies from inside the bathroom stall.

"Do you like being a big sister?"

"Yes."

"Do you help your mom with chores and cleaning up at home?"

"Sometimes."

"I wish I had a sister," Denise mutters.

"My sister always picks on me and calls me dorky."

As Cheyenne is pulling down her shorts and underwear from under her dress she notices Denise peeking through the crack between the door and the wall. She looks to make sure the door is locked and sits down on the toilet.

"You're not dorky," Denise says, looking Cheyenne in the eyes through the crack. "You look pretty in your Disney dress. Are you Cinderella?"

Cheyenne feels happy to hear that someone doesn't think she was weird. The kids didn't play with her much on the playground at recess and avoided sitting next to her at lunch. She usually sat by herself at the end of the lunch table hoping someone would come and talk to her. It was very rare that someone did, and today she feels extra alone.

"Thank you, but I *am* dorky. And my mom and my sister always call me fat."

"I think you're beautiful," Denise smiles, not taking her eyes off Cheyenne. "Are you finished?"

Cheyenne breaks from her thoughts. She can't believe that someone thinks she's beautiful. For the first time in her life she feels like Snow White, the prettiest of them all. She has never felt that way before.

"Yes. Here I come," Cheyenne says and notices that Denise is no longer in sight.

"Ms. Denise?"

"I'm here. Come on out," she whispers.

Cheyenne still can't see her. As soon as she unlocks the door, Denise pushes it open and almost hits her.

"Pull you shorts back down. I want to try something with you. I like to do this to the pretty girls," Denise says, as she is holding a large rock.

"No, we have to go back. I'm done now," Cheyenne says.

She's happy someone thinks she's beautiful but something about the look in Denise's eyes makes her feel uneasy. She starts to sweat, causing her glasses to slide down her nose.

"This will be quick," Denise promises. "Mrs. Libby knows you're with me, so you won't get in trouble."

"*No!*" Cheyenne yells.

Denise yanks Cheyenne's shorts down to her ankles, bends her over, and inserts the rock and what feels like sticks into Cheyenne's private area. She tries to pull back but there is nowhere to go.

"*No! Leave me alone!*"

Denise uses even more force and tells Cheyenne she better be quiet or it's going to hurt worse. Cheyenne cries silently as Denise sticks objects in her. Overwhelmed by pain, she eventually zones out.

When she's finished, Denise warns Cheyenne not to say a word to anyone and calmly walks her back to the classroom like nothing just happened. Cheyenne keeps the secret because she's afraid she'll be teased more. But she cries on the inside because she knows this was not supposed to happen.

Chapter 2

Stanley had decided to pick his daughter up from school instead of having her ride the bus home. He comes to the school expecting to see a happy little girl and hear all about her day. But instead he's greeted with a solemn girl who looks like she's had her worst day ever.

"How was your day Cheyenne?" Stanley asks Cheyenne as she slowly gets into the car. "You look so pretty."

"Daddy, Denise did something to me in the bathroom."

"What did you say, Chi?" Stanley asks.

Cheyenne starts crying hysterically unable to get a word out. She feels scared and hides her face in her hands.

"It's my fault, Daddy. She said I was beautiful."

Stanley immediately pulls the car over and hugs his daughter trying to fight back his anger. *Did someone just violate my baby girl?* The thought sends him into a rage and he punches the front windshield of his car.

I'm going to kill her, he silently swears, blood oozing from his hand. To his daughter, he asks gently, "Cheyenne, what did she do sweetheart?"

Cheyenne can only scream and cry. Stanley knows without doubt someone has taken advantage of his daughter because he can see the shame in her eyes.

"I'm going to handle this. Don't you worry."

I'm going to hurt somebody. Stanley puts the car in drive and heads back to the school. *You put your hands on my baby, be ready for me to put my hands on you,* Stanley thinks, a tear rolling down his cheek. He can't help but blame himself for not protecting his daughter. *I should have protected her* was all he could think about. *How could I let this happen?*

Cheyenne is running for her life as three girls are chasing her. She feels like her life will be over if she is caught. She has never been this scared in her life. The girls yell for her to bring her little ugly butt here and tell her to stop running so they can have their fun with her. They finally catch her and she has to fight for her life. They pull on her clothes, rip her dress, and scratch her body. She is crying for someone to save her...
She wakes up and her bed is soaking wet. Again.

Although the teacher's assistant was expelled from the school and sent to jail, Cheyenne never found peace. The media coverage was like a big circus act and she felt as if it was her fault. Her dad was there to console her but her mom didn't want her co-workers to get all riled up about it so she swept it under the rug. That was her best way of handling it.

"I should have never told anyone what happened." Cheyenne tells Shanice as they play jacks on the playground.

"Why?"

"Because now I feel weird, and everyone looks at me more funny, and I keep having bad dreams at night."

"About your prince?"

"No, an evil witch," Cheyenne says solemnly. "She touches me."

Shanice is silent.

"She touches my privates," Cheyenne says

Shanice has a puzzled look on her face. *Privates?*

"And she pushes me and calls me names and is being mean. I kicked her in my dream, but she just wouldn't leave me alone."

"Well, don't tell anyone. It'll go away," Shanice says. "Let's go watch them play soccer."

They run over to the grass and watch the kids play soccer. No one asks if they want to join in. Cheyenne kicks rocks thinking about Ms. Denise, wishing that had never happened and that her prince would show up and be nice again.

I want my prince. He will protect me, Cheyenne thinks. *I never had my ball. God, please bring me my prince.*

Chapter 3

Cheyenne grows into a quiet and reserved teenager. She keeps everything to herself. When she does share any bit of how she's feeling, she shares it with the wrong people. She never wants to share her deepest feelings because she doesn't trust anymore. All her faith and trust is in God and she reads her Bible every evening before she goes to bed. This is where she finds her solitude and her only real security.

Cheyenne and her family attend Northern Star Church every single Sunday and Bible study on Wednesdays. They never miss a service. Her parents are keen on raising their girls with the Lord and Savior in their lives. They would know God and live by His word.

"Cheyenne, you need to start wearing a bra baby. You are changing into a young woman now," one of the church ladies says after service.

Cheyenne is only 13, but she's becoming a little lady: thinning up and filling out—and getting more attention. Boys want to hug her and have started asking to take her out. She's also getting a few looks. She feels a sense of empowerment. Everything that happened to her had come and gone, except at night in her sleep when she's reminded of her stolen innocence.

She begins to care about her appearance. She wants to keep up with the latest, trendy hip-hop fashions that she sees New York rappers and her favorite singers wearing on TV. (Her mother complains her pants are too short at least fifty times a week.) She had asked her mother if she could get her hair cut into an asymmetrical bob, the latest hair style next to thick, long braids for the urban girls, but her mom said no. Cheyenne was mad because her mother said no but she still likes her look. Cheyenne also likes the attention it brings but still keeps to herself. Her sister makes her feel a little funny about her new body and new style, but she tries her best to ignore it.

Cheyenne and Shanice are the best of friends. Once they got into the ninth grade, Cheyenne's mom would let her go over to Shanice's house after school. Shanice's mom, Cherry, is cool. It's okay to cuss, hang out outside with boys, and not do homework. Her mom is pre-occupied with the men she tends to, her beer, and cigarettes.

Shanice and Cheyenne are inseparable in high school. They even wear matching outfits. They make friends and hang out with neighborhood kids who go to alternative school, meaning they got kicked out of regular school for bad attendance or behavior. But they are mad cool, easy going, and laugh all the time as if they don't have a care in the world.

Cheyenne is used to being in a stuffy household, where her parents are cordial but don't really talk much to each other. When they do it's always her mom talking down to her dad, mainly telling him what he better do.

Cheyenne can go around the block to Shanice's and just let her hair down and have some freedom. Shanice's mom is funny and teases the girls about boys and sex.

"Ya'll don't end up like me: single with no good man. Keep your head up, eyes open, and legs closed. You hear me?" She says this just about every day.

"We know mom. We know," the girls assure her.

"I'm serious. These boys ain't about nothin'. They just want booty, drink, and money. Don't fall for it."

Yet, all Cheyenne ever sees her doing is hanging onto guys who seem like they want the same thing—women, liquor, and money.

Cheyenne thinks she chooses not to follow her own rules but is good at giving them out. The guys she dates are unattractive and wear dingy clothes and none of them have cars. But they always came to Cherry for some fun and a good time. She feeds them and lets them lay on her couch while she talks on the phone to her girlfriends about someone else's man in the neighborhood.

Cheyenne and her family had moved out of their apartment once Felicia and Stanley earned their college degrees and got better paying jobs. They were able to buy a nice, four-bedroom home nearby so Cheyenne and Patrice didn't have to change schools. However, their new neighborhood that was once good had started to turn a little bad. Gang members now sold drugs about four blocks down from where they lived.

A lot of the moms around Shanice's neighborhood have drug dealing boyfriends or gang members as close friends. These women would rather have a man in the street versus a man who works a regular job. They admired the fast money. The ladies and the girls see these men as more valuable and attractive. Even Shanice and Cheyenne like them because they always have nice cars, new shoes, and fresh haircuts. They always pull out money and buy the little kids ice cream in the summer.

Truth be told, all these single ladies are just looking to be saved. When that E-40 song came out, "Captain Save a Hoe," all the ladies sung it.

I wanna be saved...

It's crazy to watch the difference between the people who work and go to church and the ones who don't.

The ladies in church always have something to say to Cheyenne. They're always in her business. "You better stay away from those devil boys on the streets. You need to repent."

It's funny how we can be attracted to the opposite of how we are brought up, Cheyenne thinks. But in the back of her mind she always remembers how her pastor says that you must be equally yoked.

Shanice loves that Cheyenne's parents are still together and that there isn't any drama at her house. It's peaceful, and the only people who visit are from their church for Bible study. Felicia, now a church minister, cooks every night and they sit down and eat dinner as a family. Shanice loves being in that environment and secretly craves it for herself. She once admitted to Cheyenne of being a little jealous because her mom was loud and brought any and everybody into their home. Shanice thinks her friend's family life is great. It's her personal escape.

Shanice was invited to a day party and wanted to go because Charles Dimples would be there. He's the cutest boy she's ever seen and she hears he has a lot of money, which excites Shanice even more. He's a lot older than Shanice but she just wants to look at him and pinch his little dimples.

Shanice wrote Cheyenne a note asking if she wants to skip school and go. She said they would dance, meet some new people then get back home by their regular time and their parents would never know.

Cheyenne agreed.

When they get to Charissa's house there is at least 50 people there, the music is loud and everyone is laughing and having a good time. All the guys are in red and the girls have on short shorts and brown lip liner with lip gloss. Most of the girls have already graduated from high school so Shanice and Cheyenne agree to lie about their age.

"Hey, you want a drink?" a young lady asks and hands Cheyenne and Shanice red Solo cups.

Cheyenne looks around and notices a very handsome man is staring at her while someone is talking to him. They make eye contact and Cheyenne takes a sip of her drink for the first time to take her attention off of him.

She takes a big gulp of her drink and nearly spit it out. It tasted horrible.

"What is this?" she asks no one.

"It's beer, girl!" Shanice says, moving her body to the beat of the pumping bass, taking another sip of her drink.

Cheyenne follows her lead and drinks from her plastic cup. She can't help but notice this tall, dark, and handsome guy staring at her. He smiles and nods, gesturing her to come over to where he's standing. Cheyenne is too scared so she acts like she didn't see his invitation, puts her drink on the nearest table, and starts dancing with the girl who gave her the drink.

"It's getting hot in here…" played loud from the stereo system and set the ambiance. After four songs Shanice walks over to Cheyenne. "Aye, this guy wants to meet you."

"Who?"

"Girl, he is fine and you need to come meet him. He's friends with Charles Dimples."

"Okay, okay." Cheyenne takes another sip of her drink and takes hold of Shanice's hand as they maneuver through the packed crowd. Cheyenne is nervous. She has seen this guy before at the barber shop while there with her dad. She thought he was cute, but today he looks extra fine. When she gets up close and he smiles at her she feels something she's never felt before: desire.

"Hey, you saw me looking at you. Why you don't come over here?" this tall, chocolate man asks.

"I didn't see you," Cheyenne lies, blushing.

"Aye…let's go outside so I can talk to you. You okay with that?"

Cheyenne nods and follows him out to the back yard.

"So what's your name?" he asks

"Cheyenne," she says slowly.

"Cheyenne...I like that. I'm going to call you Chi. I'm from Chicago but have been in Virginia most of my life, but the Chi is still in me," he says, putting his fist to his heart.

Cheyenne is admiring his every movement. There is something about him she likes.

"You want to get in me?" he asks.

"Huh?"

"You want to get in me? Get to know me? I want to get to know Cheyenne." He touches her left shoulder gently.

Chills go down her spine. "How can I do that? Where do you live? You live around here?" Cheyenne asks him.

"Naw, I live in the Flats," he says, referring to a rougher side of town her parents forbid her to go alone. "But I get around."

"Okay. So why do you want to get to know me?" Cheyenne asks.

"Because I like you. You seem real genuine. Not like these other hoes."

"Why do you have to call them hoes?" Cheyenne asks, offended.

"Because that's how they act: like hoes," he says with no apology. "But you though...I can tell you're not like them. You're different. I've seen you a few times on the block," he adds. "I can see you don't have no man. You keep to yourself. You're not messy like half these girls. I know a real woman when I see one."

"Oh, really?" Cheyenne smiles.

"Yup. So let me get to know you and take you somewhere."

Is he asking me out on a real date? Cheyenne has never been asked out on a real date before. She's flattered and feels special, and convinces herself he's probably never taken out any other girls before.

"Okay, I guess we can," she says.

"We can what?"

"Go out."

"Oh, you want me to take you on a date?" he chuckles. "I knew you are different. Okay, what you doing on Saturday?"

Cheyenne's mind is a little crazy right now. "Nothing."

"Okay, let's meet at the Rink at six o'clock. You good with that?"

"Yes."

"Let me give you my cell number just in case you need to reach me. Call me after 9:00."

She gives him her phone and he types in the number. He gently takes her hand and kisses it. "It was a pleasure meeting you Ms. Chi."

She looked in his hazel eyes. "You too. So what's your name?"

"Lamar."

"Okay. Bye, Lamar. I'm going to go home and help my sister with her homework now," she says with a big smile.

"See, I knew you are different. I can guarantee you none of these hoes in here is helping somebody with they homework."

They both laugh.

She turns and walks away.

Lamar says to his boy who walks by, "I hit the jackpot, homie!"

His friend gives him dap and they walk back into the house.

It takes Cheyenne some time to locate Shanice, who's hugged up with Charles Dimples. They look like they've known each other for years even though this is their first time actually speaking to each other.

"Hey, girl. I have to go and I don't want to leave you here. We came together so we leave together," Cheyenne says to her intoxicated friend.

"Okay, just give me five minutes," Shanice says.

While waiting Cheyenne can't stop thinking about Lamar. *I wonder how old he is. What is his mom like? Is he a good kisser (even though she has never kissed a boy before)? What does he do for a living? I wonder does he believe in God? Why did he ask me out? What makes me so special?*

She is going over everything in her mind until Shanice taps her on her shoulder. "Come on girl, let's go."

No, no, no, no, no! Leave me alone! I don't want to. Just stop. I'm so sick of this. Why did you do this to me? I am going to get my dad to kill you. You messed with the wrong one. I am not the one. Leave me alone...

Cheyenne wakes up with urine in her bed. Again.

Chapter 4

Cheyenne doesn't know how she's going to convince her parents to let her out at 6:00 p.m. on a Saturday night, so she asks her dad if she can spend the night over Shanice's. She tells him it's their friend's birthday and they are having a group sleepover at Shanice's house. Her dad agrees because he trusts his oldest child, but Patrice isn't buying it.

"You know are you lying!" she says so their dad can hear.

"Shut up, girl. You are always in my business. Can I have a life without you worrying about me?"

"I'm going to ask Mom if I can go too since it's a girls' night out. I want to hang out with the girls too," Patrice says.

"No, you don't need to come. You're too young and you will spoil a good night," Cheyenne says as she pushes her 14-year-old sister—who is now taller than her—out of her way.

"You're always trying to rain on my parade," Cheyenne barks at her sister.

"So what?" Patrice pauses. "Well have fun, Sis."

"I will," she smiles.

It takes Cheyenne an hour to decide what to wear for her date with Lamar. She imagined what he'd be wearing, how he'd make her feel, what they'd do as she pranced around her bedroom, singing Ja Rule's, "Put It on Me."

> *Where would I be without you (uh)*
> *I only think about you (yeah)*

I know you're tired or being lonely (lonely)
So baby girl put it on me (put it on me)

Cheyenne reaches to grab her shoes from the top of her closet and the tiara from her Disney princess outfit falls to the floor. She picks it up, runs to her bathroom, and places it gently and perfectly on her head.

"I am a princess today," she says while looking at herself in the mirror for the few minutes.

She immediately recalls a dream she had as a child: A tall, dark man with pretty eyes picking her up. She was wearing a big, blue gown. He told her, "I got you."

She smiles, takes off her tiara, and places it on her bathroom counter. She looks at herself one last time to make sure her hair is just right, her Apple Bottom jeans are fitting tight, and her Baby Phat top is perfectly showing her belly button. She looks down at her fly heels, puts her gold hoops in, and heads out the door.

"Bye, Mom. Bye, Dad. I'll call you later." She slams the door without waiting for their reply.

"That girl is something else. I'm glad to see she is happy now. I thought she'd never get passed what happened." Felicia tells Stanley. "You know she is still wetting the bed. She doesn't think I know, but I smell it. She changes the sheets on her bed before I have to tell her to."

"Let's hope she stops that soon. I think she will forget it and grow out of it," Stanley says.

"I'm praying she does," Felicia sighs.

Stanley gets up and returns with the Holy Bible to kneel and pray with his wife.

"Father, we come to you today asking for your protection over our child's life. To cover her with the blood. Guide and use her for your glory. Protect my family, Lord. Amen."

"I was thinking we go out and do something different tonight. Call Bernice and see if she can stay here with Patrice. I don't want to leave her here alone," Stanley says to his wife.

"What did you have in mind?" Felicia asks, excited about being alone with her husband. They haven't been on a date in years.

"I don't know. I just want to go relax and do something with you. We've been working so hard worrying about these girls and the church. I want us to do something," Stanley says.

Felicia smiles brightly. She's flattered and blushes at her husband making such bold attempts to keep her happy. She considers herself the backbone of the family and is tired of always being the one to come up with things for the family to do and having to solve all the problems because her husband never steps up, in her opinion.

"Okay, well you think of something and I'll call Bernice. My sister loves coming over here to eat up my food anyway, and Cheyenne don't even touch her plate," Felicia says as she picks up the big yellow phone nailed to the wall in their kitchen.

⚜⚜⚜

Cheyenne pays her own way and walks into The Rink a little past six o'clock. She doesn't want to get there right on time. She wants Lamar to wait for her. Once inside she searches for him but does not see him anywhere. She decides to sit in the front so that when he walks in he can see her right away.

Fifteen minutes go by and she wonders if he's going to stand her up. She pulls out his cell number from her purse and calls him, but he does not answer but he calls back in under a minute.

"Hey, Chi," he says.

"Hey."

"Where are you? I'm out here waiting for you at The Rink," Lamar says anxiously.

"I'm inside."

"What! Oh man, okay I'll be right there."

Lamar walks in looking like a rich rap star. He is wearing a big gold cross medallion, red Coogie shirt, and big gold watch with his pants hanging slightly from his waist. He catches the attention of many girls and nods to a few of them but focuses on who he came to see.

"Hi, Lamar," says a woman who looks to be in her 30s with a twinkle in her eyes as he breezes past her.

"What's good, Lamar?" a man asks giving a secret hand gesture.

"Hey, Lamar," a group of young teenagers say in unison as he gets closer to Cheyenne. He nods and smiles to the girls out of respect.

When he reaches the bench where Cheyenne is sitting, Lamar picks her up and wraps her in a great big hug.

"I'm going to have to teach you how to let a man take care of you. You don't have to pay to come in here," he says.

"Oh, I didn't know. I'm sorry," Cheyenne says.

Lamar reached into his pockets and pulls out a big wad of hundreds and twenties wrapped in a rubber band. He hands Cheyenne a twenty-dollar bill.

"Here. Don't ever reach into your purse when you are with me," Lamar says. "I got you."

Cheyenne goes into dream state. She smiles, thanks him, and takes the money. "Let me see what you're working with on these skates."

"You don't want none," Lamar jokes as he gets up to go get his skates.

They laugh and enjoy each other's company the entire night. Cheyenne learns that Lamar lives with his mother, has a younger sister, and an older brother in jail. His dad was murdered by a cop after a bar fight he was a victim of in another state. Lamar likes to do wild things, loves animals and cars, hang with his boys, smokes a little reefer, and plays craps.

Lamar is enjoying Cheyenne's company too. He starts to think that she may be out of his league because she does not drink, smoke, or cuss; comes from a good home with two parents who are financially well off; and she is a virgin. He's determined to be himself because he really likes her and doesn't want any other guy in the streets to get their hands on her. He wants her all to himself. He needs a good, young woman he can train to hold him down. He is making headway in his drug operation and making some good contacts. He has some work to do in upstate New York that is risky but will come with large benefits. As a gang member with the Bloods, there is a lot of pressure to stay on top and make money so people will respect you and know not to mess with you.

Lamar is already planning his life with Cheyenne. She is his perfect girl.

Coincidently, Stanley and Felicia make their way to the skating rink for some old-time fun. They are having a ball, laughing and reminiscing about their childhood days when they used to sneak and meet at this very same place. Stanley used to save his money up so he could buy his special lady—who he thought was the prettiest girl in school—popcorn and soda. All he wanted to do was impress her so she would only want him. All the guys wanted her attention. He was lucky he had it and made the most of it.

Felicia reminded Stanley that the rink was where they shared their first kiss.

"Like this?" Stanley surprises her with a kiss on the lips.

She giggles and says, "Yeah, and you still need help in that department."

"Yeah, whatever. You didn't say that then," he says with confidence.

She smiles and grabs his hand as they skate for a little while.

Luckily, Cheyenne and Lamar decide to leave early because they wanted to listen to some music together in Lamar's car and talk. Their evening was perfect also. They laughed the entire evening. Cheyenne loves to laugh and Lamar sure knows how to make her smile. She is smitten. It's just like a fairy tale. Perfect.

Chapter 5

Cheyenne gets to Shanice's house around eleven o'clock. She gently knocks on her bedroom window from the backyard to tell her to come open the front door.

"Girl, I really like Lamar," Cheyenne shares with her best friend once she gets inside her room.

"You do? What did you guys do?" Shanice asks sitting down on her bed.

Cheyenne shares their entire evening. "He opened the door for me. He says: *I got you.* He is so nice."

Shanice congratulates her friend and wishes them the best. "I really hope it works out for you two. You think he will be your first?"

"No, I'm not ready for that until I get married. I really don't want that kind of relationship until I'm mature enough to handle it."

"You know he's going to ask," Shanice says.

"I know, but I did tell him I was a virgin, and he will have to wait until I'm ready. He says he's cool with that, and he'll wait for as long as he has to. He says he really digs me, and I'm worth waiting for."

"Well then, he's probably going to get it from one of these other skanks if you make him wait too long," Shanice warns Cheyenne.

Cheyenne lets that thought of Lamar with another girl process in her head for a moment. "Well then, he's not the one for me," she says with confidence. "*But because of the temptation to sexual immorality, each man should have his own wife and each woman her own husband*," Cheyenne recites from 1 Corinthians 7:2.

Shanice shakes her head, turns off her lamp, and gets under the covers. "Yeah, okay, sure."

Cheyenne falls into a deep slumber as she lays next to Shanice in her bed. She can't get Lamar off her mind. This is the first boy who has showed real interest in her, and she believes they have a future together.

"He got me," she whispers in her sleep. "He got me."

As Cheyenne lays on Lamar's chest unclothed he tells her he loves every single inch of her and kisses her forehead. Cheyenne kisses his bare shoulder as she lays in bed with her prince and says, 'I love you too.'

⚜ ⚜ ⚜

"I want you to meet my mom," Lamar says, looking in Cheyenne's eyes after he finishes chewing his fries.

She freezes from taking a sip from her soda. They are at the Cook Out Restaurant eating dinner.

"Really? Okay. When?" Cheyenne asks.

"After I get back in town this weekend. Is that cool?" he asks.

"Yeah, sure."

Lamar has been going out of town once a week, driving up to Jersey to handle his business. Cheyenne has also noticed his name being brought up in some local gang fights and she's seen scratches and bruises on his arms and neck. But she never questions his whereabouts. She figures if he wants her to know, he will tell her. But she is convinced and secure that he is taking care of business because he calls her every night, checks on her, and tells her he loves her and only her. When home he sneaks into her house after she gets home from school because her dad is working longer hours and her mom doesn't get home until 8:00 p.m. on most nights. Patrice keeps her mouth shut because she's having boys over too.

Now, they are definitely taking things to the next level because she is going to meet Lamar's mom who he admires, loves, and respects. He says if anyone ever tried to harm his mother, he would kill them.

Cheyenne and Lamar are spending every single moment of their free time together. She wishes he would go to church, but doubts that will ever happen.

Lamar is very familiar with the streets but he also knows how to treat a lady. He's 20 years old, four years Cheyenne's senior, so he knew how to be her man. He cares so much about her and truly values their relationship.

Cheyenne learned from her mother how *not* to treat a man. Her mother is very forceful and demanding with her dad and she can see that her dad doesn't really like that type of treatment, so she vowed to not belittle Lamar or ever speak down on him.

At their family cook outs she watches how older married women treat their men. They smile at them, fix their plates, and basically treat them like kings. She wants to be that queen for Lamar and Lamar knows it. And he loves it.

Every woman he'd ever dated or spent his time with wanted him for either sex or money. He has finally found a girl who doesn't want either from him—just his love and attention.

One day a guy from Cheyenne's school calls to see when their group was going to get together for their history project. Lamar hears a male's voice on the other end, roughly grabs the phone from Cheyenne, and threatens the young boy until he hangs up.

Cheyenne asks, "Why did you do that?

"Because I don't' want no dudes calling you—ever! I don't care what it's about. You have them call me if they want to talk to you."

Cheyenne sighs. She can't believe her ears, but she obliges. This is her king, so she'll obey. She hugs Lamar from the back and massages his shoulders and tells him it will never happen again. She kisses his neck.

Lamar pushes her off. "You can't be doing that if you're not going to open up those legs for me."

Cheyenne put her head down because she's heard this kind of talk over the last few months from Lamar. She knew what was coming next.

"So when are you going to see that I'm that man who should get it?" Lamar asks. "Are you saving it for someone else? I got plenty of girls out here who want me to have theirs, so what's up, Chi? When is it going to be time? I come over here every day and you tease me."

He gets up to lock her bedroom door.

"Lamar, I'm just not ready. I want to be married or at least engaged. I'm only 16," she tries to explain.

"Look, it's been seven months. I can't take it anymore," Lamar says as he walks towards her.

Cheyenne sees a hungry look in his eyes she's never seen before. "Lamar, when the time—"

In that instant Lamar pins both of her arms down to her bed with one hand and uses the other to unbutton, unzip, and tear off her shorts.

She yells for him to stop, but he only gets more aggressive.

"I love you, Cheyenne. I'm tired of waiting," Lamar says, pressing the full weight of his 175 pounds onto her, sliding his hand between her legs. "You are ready, girl."

"No, I swear I don't want this. Please, get up Lamar! Please! I don't want this!"

Lamar puts a pillow over her mouth and inserts himself into her, ignoring her muffled screams. Cheyenne is fighting and pulling back trying to get out from under him, but she can't move and the pain is making everything worse. He body goes into shock and she becomes numb. Lamar rhythmically thrusts himself into her, moaning and saying how much he loves her.

"Calm down. I got you, Chi. Be quiet. I'm almost finished."

Cheyenne closes her eyes waiting for this pain to end.

Lamar moans louder. "I love you, Cheyenne."

"Stop!" Cheyenne screams from under the pillow. "Just stop!"

Lamar doesn't stop. He rams his body into hers forcedly as he tells her he couldn't wait and that he loves her. Cheyenne's numb body just lays still until he finishes.

Chapter 6

A woman is breathing hard and running towards
Cheyenne with her clothes ripped from her body. Cheyenne sees
panic in her face and asks the lady if she needs some help. The
lady looks at Cheyenne as if she is going to harm her. Cheyenne
assures her that she is there to help, grabs her hand and runs
with her. They both look back and three men are chasing them.
They run faster and faster, and the lady ends up falling.
Cheyenne picks her up and tells her she has to run and that she
won't let anything happen to her. Cheyenne tells the woman
that she is there to protect her from getting hurt, but the woman
refuses to get up. Cheyenne tries with all her might to lift the
woman but the woman won't budge. Cheyenne starts punching
her and begging her to get up telling her she can't let this happen
to her. Begging her to get up or else. The woman looks at
Cheyenne and says she's tired of running and gives up...

Cheyenne keeps quiet around the house and stays away from
Shanice. She had finally stopped wetting the bed but every night
for the last week since Lamar forced himself on her, she has been
wetting the bed in her sleep again.

"Cheyenne, are you okay honey?" Felicia asks one early
Saturday morning.

"Yes, just tired and can't wait until summer," Cheyenne lies.

"Honey, I noticed your wet sheets. Do you want to talk
about it?"

Cheyenne is so embarrassed. "It just happened mom. I had a bad dream. Shanice and I were watching scary movies, and I think I got scared and had an accident. It's nothing."

"Okay. Well, I have to get to a church planning meeting, but if you want to talk I'm here, okay?"

Felicia rubs her daughter's shoulder gently, recites a Bible verse letting her know that God will take care of it, and just pray.

"I need you to be strong so you can get an education and be successful in life. You can't let things hold you back. I want you to become somebody, like me. You don't necessarily have to become a minister, but I do want you to get into hospitality so you can help people, okay? Don't allow what happened in the past keep you from your future," Felicia warns then leaves to go to church for work.

Cheyenne has not returned Lamar's phone calls and has not spoken to her best friend either. She picks up the phone to invite Shanice over. Shanice misses her friend and arrives in no time. They shoot the breeze, drink some lemonade, and turn some music on in Cheyenne's room.

"Girl, look at these new kicks Damian bought me." Shanice bends her right leg to show off her sneakers.

Cheyenne looks down. "Those are dope. So who is Damian?"

"He is this sucka with a lot of dough. His family owns like three car dealerships, and they have mad bank. He buys me whatever I want. You know I don't mess with no broke dudes." Shanice snaps her fingers, thrusts her hips out, and laughs.

"Yea, I know," Cheyenne says.

"Girl, you can tell these dudes anything. Remember that guy who Nicki was seeing?"

Cheyenne nods even though she doesn't remember.

Shanice goes on. "He dumped her and was trying to get with me. I told him he has to pay what he weighs."

The both laugh. Shanice loves a guy who will spend money on her and never stays with anyone for that long. She likes them older, rough around the edges, and with money to spend on her. Cheyenne is way too shy to ask Lamar for money. That just won't happen.

"So what's up with you and L-Boogie? That is your Boo!" Shanice says with a big smile. "I'm so happy for you, girl. You have found love. I haven't heard about him with nobody. But girls do be checking for him though."

"We are cool," Cheyenne says dully.

"Just cool? Ya'll are like Bonnie and Clyde."

"I wouldn't say all that," Cheyenne says with an attitude.

Shanice looks her friend in the eyes. "Uh-oh, girl. What happened? He cheated on you?"

Cheyenne readjusts herself in her seat next to her desk. "No, he raped me." She starts to cry.

Shanice stands up. "What! Get out of here! What!" She grabs her friend's hands and kneels in front of her. "Are you okay? How did this happen? Have you spoke to him? You tell anyone? Oh my, God, I'm so sorry."

Cheyenne just keeps crying.

"It's okay, Chi. It's not your fault."

"I could have stopped him, but I was so in shock that he was taking advantage of me and demanding that I have sex with him."

"He's a chump. I can't stand him for this. I feel so bad because I introduced ya'll. Ugh! I'm so pissed! I'm sorry, girl." Shanice is so ticked and hurts for her friend. She can't imagine what she is going through but needs to be there for her.

"I feel so bad," Cheyenne says.

"You shouldn't."

"I'm no longer a virgin. I didn't want my first time to be like this. I wanted to wait until we, well I got married. Now that's gone." Cheyenne sobs harder. "Why does this always have to happen to me? What did I do, God?" she cries out, looking up towards heaven. "God, please destroy this devil who is trying to destroy me. I promise I will live by Your word. I promise God."

"Cheyenne, God loves you. Stay strong. I need you to stay strong, so we can get through this. Everything will be alright," Shanice says trying to calm her down.

"I can't take this much longer. What am I going to do?"

"You are going to keep on living and not blame yourself. He was the idiot. He is the devil and will pay for this. You don't deserve it, but you will be okay. I promise," Shanice says.

All Cheyenne could do was cry in her friend's arms until she fell asleep.

Lamar stops by unannounced for two weeks straight. Patrice always tells him Cheyenne is not home and he better be careful about coming over because he might get caught. Lamar doesn't care. He wants to see Cheyenne. He wants her back.

On the last day of Cheyenne's sophomore year, she's walking home and Lamar pulls up beside her.

"Chi!" he yells. "Chi, come here."

Cheyenne looks over at Lamar's pretty hazel eyes and walks over to the car.

"What, Lamar?"

"Get in the car."

She gets in so she can tell him face-to-face to let her be.

"Cheyenne, I promise it will never happen again. I just wanted you so bad I couldn't help myself. You do that to me, but I promise if you don't want that part of me I can wait. I really do love you with all my heart. You are my queen."

Cheyenne looks at Lamar's sincere and apologetic face and thinks about how much she's missed him. She's missed having him to lean on, tell her dreams to, and to love.

"Do you forgive me Chi, baby?" Lamar begs and pulls out flowers and a wrapped gift.

"Yes, I forgive you." Cheyenne looks at him excited.

"Let me make it up to you. Let's go downtown and celebrate your last day of school."

Lamar takes her to all her favorite shops. They visit museums, laugh, and eat ice cream just like old times.

"Whose car is this?" Cheyenne finally asks.

"It's my homeboy's car. He's letting me use it for the day," Lamar says hesitantly.

Lamar kisses Cheyenne gently before he drops her off a half-block from her house. "I'm here for you Cheyenne. I'm all you need."

⚜ ⚜ ⚜

"Come in but be quiet. I don't want my sister to know you're here," Cheyenne says.

Lamar stands at the door of her house. "Just come outside and take a ride with me. I just have to see you for a few minutes," Lamar begs.

Cheyenne grabs her sweater and follows him to the car. "Whose car is this?" Cheyenne asks, noticing it's a different car from last week.

"It's Pete's. These fools let me use their rides whenever I want to go handle my business," Lamar says.

Cheyenne admires the new Lexus's plush leather seats, vinyl door handles, big sunroof, and new car smell. Lamar has some R. Kelly slow jams lightly playing in the car and she smells a whiff of marijuana. She leans back to relax and just take in the nice summer breeze, music, luxury and being with her man. Lamar leans over and kisses her passionately.

"You're so beautiful. I love you. I be missing you so much Cheyenne," he whispers between kisses.

"You know, I'm 21 now, so I have some liquor if you want some."

Cheyenne declines and pushes him back because he smells of weed and liquor. "You got to stop that. I notice every time I see you now you're either high or have been drinking."

Lamar ignores her and reaches down between her legs. Cheyenne jumps when she feels his hand on her private area again. She immediately has a flashback of this same hand aggressively entering her body. She reaches for the door. Lamar locks the door and straddles her. He kisses her in places that are forbidden.

Cheyenne feels his breath and says, "I have to leave Lamar."

Lamar pulls her panties down and leans her car seat back. Within seconds he's laying half naked on top of her. She's hitting the door trying to get out, yelling for him to leave her alone and let her go into the house. She looks out the window and sees no one in sight. She realizes screaming will not help and she does not want to get noticed in a car with a 21-year-old man.

She begs him to stop but within an instant it's too late; he is ramming and pushing and moaning, taking what he wants from her. Again.

She says, "Lamar, I thought you said you wouldn't. Please stop. No!"

"I can't help myself. I think about your body every single second. Just let me have it," Lamar says.

She is slapping and pushing him but Lamar will not let up. She notices lights coming from around the corner and says, "Lamar—my dad!"

Lamar rolls off of her and pulls his pants up. Cheyenne grabs her panties and puts them back on then manages to unlock the door and run into her house. Lamar burns rubber and takes off down the road.

♕♕♕

Luckily it is not Stanley coming down the street but a neighbor, but Cheyenne is able to get out of the car before Lamar can finish violating her.

She goes to her room, throws her clothes on the floor, and notices blood in her underwear. She takes a shower and cries in shame. She can't believe she let this happen again.

Three full days go by and surprisingly Lamar has not tried to call Cheyenne.

"Patrice has Lamar called me?" Cheyenne asks

"No, not that I know of."

"Cheyenne, come here. Let me talk to you," her dad yells from the garage.

It sounds like she's in trouble, but she's looking forward to talking to her dad. Her mom has been so busy at the church and he has been keeping himself busy working on cars and fixing anything he could get his hands on.

They used to talk a lot before she started dating Lamar. He would encourage her to get good grades, stay away from boys who did not deserve her, to value herself as a woman, and save herself for the right guy. Cheyenne is hoping they will have that type of conversation today because she sure needs her dad right now.

"Yes, Dad." Cheyenne sits down on a small foot stool looking at her dad under the hood of a 1976 Chevy.

Stanley puts his tools down and grabs a towel to clean his hands. "We haven't talked in a very long time, and I really regret that because I think you may have gotten yourself wrapped up into some things. I'm worried about you. You don't know this, but I saw you at the rink with that drug dealer."

Cheyenne's eyes get wide open. She looks away from her dad and goes back to that moment. *Oh my goodness, no wonder my dad and I got really close after that.*

"I don't say anything because I wanted to see how you would handle yourself. I know we've raised you right, so I thought it was a phase and if I say anything it would draw you more towards him."

Cheyenne is stunned.

"He called here collect from jail today, Cheyenne, and I had a long talk with him," Stanley says. "We prayed together, and I told him that I was not going to allow him to mess up your life. He has some things God is going to have to get him though. You can't help him with where he is right now. He needs to find himself and get right with God. That boy has a long history of drug trafficking, domestic abuse, and using drugs. If he doesn't get help he will spend his entire life in jail or be dead."

Cheyenne felt sorry for Lamar.

"Your mother and I don't want you to engage your life around a man who does not value himself because he will not value you. Keep your eyes, ears, and heart open for a man who will put you before his own needs. That's how a man shows he cares about you. He will never force you against your will. He will value you and respect you, and he will never try to hide you from his baby's mother."

"He has a kid?" Cheyenne asks, stunned.

"Yes, he does. He lives with her and the child is nine months old. He went to jail on the night you all last seen each other for possession of an armed weapon and driving a stolen car."

Cheyenne doesn't know what to say. She was completely shocked.

"Cheyenne, God kept you safe that night for a reason. He has a plan for your life. Be smart, baby girl. I love you with all my heart. You and Patrice. I will kill myself if anything happens to either one of you. You have to remember who made you and walk with your chin up. Command respect from people and never think someone has to save you from anything. Everything you need, resides right here." He touches her chest. "God will provide all the answers. Know your strength."

"Daddy, he took advantage of me that night and I was in that car with him and the liquor and I guess the gun too," Cheyenne says, almost in tears. "I was so dumb."

"No, you aren't; you are just naïve. You thought he cared for you when only he cared about himself. If he really truly cared for you he would never put you in a situation that could harm you. That's real love. A real man cherishes the ground his woman's walks on. He will never sacrifice her or her freedom for his own regards. You are young, but I want you to remember that. It's not your fault he took advantage of you. He knew what he was doing. He saw you came from a good family, had morals and values, and he wanted to take that from you so he could control your mind, body, and spirit. It's okay that you fell for it, baby. Just don't ever fall for it again. He will say he's sorry a million times—because he is—but don't believe him."

"Okay, Daddy. Thank you."

He also tells her, "I am having the number changed and you are to ask your mother to take you to the doctors to get yourself checked out."

"Daddy, I'm so glad I have a man in my life who loves me and protects me. Every girl should have a daddy like you. I need you. Thank you. Things could have been so much worse," Cheyenne says as she hugs her smelly, hard-working dad.

"It's okay, sweetie. I need you to take care of you," he points at her. "You are precious and valuable like a diamond. Don't let anyone dull your shine. You promise me?"

"Yes, Daddy," Cheyenne promises and goes back inside the house.

Chapter 7

"Curtis, can you pass this up to the teacher?" Cheyenne asks the boy sitting in front of her.

Curtis grabs the paper and smiles at her like he always does. Cheyenne notices his eyes go towards their classmate Cydney who is sitting in another row to the far right of the class. Cydney is a slender cheerleader with beautiful skin. She's one of the most popular girls in school. She's in all the clubs, plays sports, cheerleads, and her grades are impeccable. She and Cheyenne really don't speak to each other because Cheyenne doesn't associate with the popular girls in school. They seem to be in too much drama and she prefers people not knowing too much about her private life.

Cydney is looking at Curtis with sharp eyes and he just turns his body back towards the teacher. Cheyenne giggles to herself at how jealous girls can be of one another. It's so senseless. What's funny is that Cheyenne never really pays any attention to Curtis even though all the others girls at school do. He's a star athlete, very cute, and has muscles for days so Cheyenne thinks he is out of her league, and really cares not to be bothered with him.

The bell rings to end class and Cheyenne grabs her things and walks towards her locker ready to head home from school. Curtis says in a friendly and calm tone, "Hey, don't you live down the street from me?"

"Yes, I live next door to Sam and Sabrina." Cheyenne's tone is just as friendly and calm.

"How are you getting home today? You want a ride?"

"With who? You?"

"Yeah, who else?" he laughs.

Cheyenne sees no harm and says, "Yeah, cool."

As they walk towards the student parking lot they talk about their plans after they graduate in three months. Cheyenne and Curtis have always been cool to each other, but never spoke one-on-one for a long period of time.

Cheyenne shares with Curtis what she wants to do. Curtis is very smart and has academic as well as sports scholarships lined up from every college he wants to attend and then some. Cheyenne is intrigued with how intelligently he speaks and his confidence. He sounds like he has some big plans and she believes him when he says he'll accomplish all of them.

What she doesn't really care for is that he talks about himself way too much. Cheyenne thinks he feels comfortable around her because all the way home he's just talking and talking—about his goals, his family, all the attention he receives from girls, and his friends. But she feels an immediate friendly connection.

For the next month he drives her to school every day, and they ride home together when he doesn't have practice or games. They simply enjoy each other's company without really saying it to one another. The friendship just grows naturally and gradually. On the occasions when Curtis has some things to do after school, he makes sure one of his friends get her home safely. They grow really close as friends and get to know each other really well.

One day Curtis tells Cheyenne that he's afraid to go off to college and be the new guy. He's worried he won't survive where he doesn't know anyone and wants to stay home and take care of his mom. He's extremely close with his mom, who isn't married.

Boys love to protect their mothers and he doesn't feel comfortable leaving her alone with his little sisters. He loves that Cheyenne gives him confidence and motivates him to do what is best for him. He's never had that type of friendship with any girl before. He likes that about Cheyenne.

He knows she is insecure about her weight and he hates it. She's about 20 pounds overweight, but he likes it. She wears it well. He thinks it's cute when she tries to hide her belly fat with her backpack by sitting it on her lap in the car. He grabs it and puts it in the back seat. He wants her to feel safe and comfortable, and she does.

They share so many laughs during their brief drives to and from school. Cheyenne finds herself looking forward to it. Of course her parents don't mind their friendship because Curtis is a good guy. He has a lot of potential. They believed he's going to be somebody and know he comes from a good Christian home.

But Cheyenne thinks he seeks too much attention, so she never looked past them just being friends until the day Curtis told her he'd decided to attend Duke University in North Carolina, five hours away. Cheyenne immediately felt sad, like she was losing her best friend. But she was proud for him. He was going to go on and do great things. She had her own dreams of nursing to pursue. Even though he was going away she knew they would keep in touch.

Late one evening right before Cheyenne is about to go to bed her cell phone rings. "Hello?"

"Hey what's up? Are you sleep?"

"Hey Curtis. No, but I was just about to go to bed. I'm tired. What's up?"

"Oh, go ahead and go to sleep. I just wanted to tell you I have to pick you up a little early because Coach wants to talk to us in the morning," Curtis explains.

"Okay, I'll be ready," Cheyenne says and hangs up.

She has a hard time going to sleep. She had stopped the bed wetting but her dreams still kept her up tossing and turning. She feels like he had something he wanted to tell her. Should she call him back, or just see if he calls her back? Did she cut him off too soon? *Maybe I shouldn't have told him I was tired.*

She tosses and turns all night. Suddenly she realizes that she really does have strong feelings for Curtis. When she finally wakes up she sees that she missed his call. He had called back shortly after they hung up. She immediately calls him back but there's no answer.

Curtis was never one to honk his horn when he came to pick her up in the morning. He would come in and say hello to her parents and walk her to the car. On a few occasions he would open her door for her. Today was one of those days. Cheyenne, who suffers from low self-esteem, always feels safe and secure when she spends time with Curtis. He is so very different from Lamar.

They sit in the car, quiet. Something is different. Usually they would converse about any and everything but not today. Cheyenne finally breaks the silence and asks what he really wanted to say last night. He comes clean and says he wants her to be his girl and be by his side as he goes away to college. He says he will send for her when he could.

"I can't think of anyone else I would rather be with, Cheyenne." He pauses then adds, "I love you."

Cheyenne blushes and touches his hand. "I can't think of anyone...," She stops and smiles She can't control her facial expressions at this point.

"Out of all the girls that try to come at me I'd rather have you. You're real. You're beautiful on the inside and out, and having you would be a privilege," Curtis says in all sincerity.

Cheyenne is smiling so big. She's in shock. She had no idea he felt this way. She can't believe anyone, especially someone like Curtis, would ever want her. No one had ever said anything like that to her before Curtis.

She sits quietly for several minutes still in pure shock that he's just poured out his heart to her. In the back of her mind Prince Charming starts to form a face. She daydreams that he's a prince who wants to be her happily ever after.

"I love you too," she whispers.

She speaks the words so quietly that Curtis doesn't hear her so she works up enough courage to say it again. "I love you too!"

"Goodness woman, you screamed that!" Curtis smiles.

Cheyenne was so nervous that she hadn't even realized how loud she said it.

"It's okay if you want to shout it to the world." Curtis says as he rubs her hand.

She blushes. "I didn't mean to say it that loud. Gosh."

An awkward silence comes upon her suddenly as she thinks back on Lamar. "Curtis."

"Yes, baby."

"Don't hurt me."

"I would never do that."

"Promise?"

"Cross my heart."

Chapter 8

It was Friday so after school they go on their first official date as girlfriend and boyfriend to the bowling alley to play pool and video games. A real Prince Charming he is. All they do is laugh. Cheyenne has never felt as happy or safe as she feels in his presence.

The next week at school, girls give her the eye and classmates who had never spoken to her before ask if she and Curtis are dating. They tell her that they too dated Curtis and to back off. Cheyenne can't find it in her heart to believe them. She is with him all the time and he talked about those girls to her and how silly they are before they even started dating. So Cheyenne just blows them off and thinks they are just jealous.

Her relationship with Curtis is blissful. They spend a lot of time at school and even after school together. They study together because Curtis is serious about his education. He loves learning and Cheyenne can see him being a good father one day. They talk about getting married and having kids.

Cheyenne and her family are in the living room one evening and Stanley asks Cheyenne how everything is going in her life.

"Everything's going good. I can't wait to go to college, get married to Curtis, and live happily ever after," Cheyenne gleams.

Cheyenne's dad just lets her talk but her mother is not having that.

"You need to be focused on your schooling. These boys will come and they will go," she says.

"Now why do you want to tell her that for, Felicia?" Stanley asks politely but pointedly.

"Because she needs to focus on herself and not that boy."

"Mom, we are just talking about it. It's not for sure yet," Cheyenne reassures her parents.

Cheyenne could never really share any good news with her mom because she always tended to turn something good into something negative. Although her dad seemed sad most of the time, he was the complete opposite. Stanley let his girls feel excitement and hopeful about any of their dreams no matter how foolish or unrealistic they sounded. It makes him feel good to hear excitement in their voices. He wants his girls to be happy, not miserable like he felt.

Stanley and Felicia still argued amongst themselves most of the time. They would fight about nothing really. Felicia always talked down on him, saying he was spending too much time away from home and in the church as a volunteer deacon. She was always breathing down his back.

He puts up with it because he doesn't want to fail his children. He had made a promise to himself that he would never leave them. Stanley knows what it was like to not live with a father so he has sacrificed his own happiness just so he can be there for his children without any fuss. There had been many nights he literally wanted to kill himself. He has really thought about it a few times too many but just can't go through with it. He often thinks that killing himself would ease his pain from his wife who he felt was ungrateful, but he can't bear the thought of leaving his daughters.

"My mom gets on my nerves," Cheyenne says to Curtis on their date at a friend's birthday party.

"Don't let it get you down," he says.

"I swear she thinks you are like Lamar. She always brings up my insecurities. I know she means well, but that was a very painful part of my life, and it wasn't even really that long ago. I feel like she keeps wanting to bring it up over and over again."

"Don't worry about that. She's trying to protect you. I don't blame her. I got your back and I wouldn't ever cross those boundaries like that idiot did. He was a clown. I don't know him, but I heard of him, and we are different. Your mom has nothing to worry about. I am in this with you forever," Curtis says then kisses her gently.

"That makes me feel better. I have to admit I do have some insecurities with myself. These little girls at school are always saying they have been with you. I don't believe them, but I can't help but feel a certain way about it," Cheyenne tells him.

"Those girls just wish they had me. I put you on a pedestal and they wish the guys they dated did that. They just want what they can't have. Don't fall for it," Curtis says

"Well look at you. You look like LL Cool J! Who wouldn't want you? I feel I don't deserve you sometimes," she admits.

"What? I'm all yours. Let's go so I can get home and watch the Wizards beat up on Houston." Curtis is serious about his basketball games.

He drops her off at home, and goes to Cydney's house to watch the game.

Chapter 9

Shanice loves to cook. She can make some good burgers and homemade fries. She and Cheyenne are eating after school in Shanice's kitchen waiting for *106 & Park* to come on so they can check out the latest music videos. The doorbell rings; it's Brittney, one of their home girls who lives nearby.

They are talking, eating, drinking soda, and watching videos. Brittney, who Cheyenne knew to hang around Cydney, starts asking questions about her and Curtis.

"So, are you guys getting serious? I see you two all hugged up all the time."

"Who?" Cheyenne asks with a proud smirk. "We've been talking about it, but I don't have no ring," Cheyenne says as she tosses her left hand in the air. Although Cheyenne is educated and uses good grammar most of the time, she often tries to fit in when around her friends, but they know she's just being goofy.

They all laugh.

"You guys will make some pretty babies," Shanice says.

"I'm sure his daughter with Cydney will be super-cute when she has it," Brittany says. "I know their daughter is going to be C.U.T.E."

It gets dead silent and Shanice looks at Cheyenne who is looking at Brittany like she wants to kill her.

"What did you just say?" Cheyenne asks slowly.

"You don't know? Cee didn't tell you?"

"Tell me what? And who is Cee?"

"Curtis. That's what we call him," Brittany explains.

"Cydney thinks she's having a baby by Curtis? That girl is delusional. She wants my man so bad she will say anything. Curtis is waiting until he is married before he has sex. What does she even think she is talking about?" Cheyenne says, sticking up for her boyfriend.

Shanice doesn't know what to say. She has heard that Cydney and Curtis have been hanging out but she knows that people like to talk a lot and doesn't believe the hype.

"That's your home girl, right? Call her. I want to hear her say it," Shanice demands. "And put her on speaker phone."

Brittany grabs her phone and calls her friend.

"Hello?" Cydney answers.

"Hey, girl. What you doing?" Brittany asks.

Loud and clear for everyone to hear she says, "Nothing girl. Sitting up here waiting for Curtis to come bring me to the hospital."

"Why are you guys going there?" Brittany asks looking at Cheyenne's sullen face.

"Girl, you know why. We have to go check on the baby."

Cheyenne's face drops as though a loved one has just died. Even though she wants to burst into tears at the moment, her pride will not allow it. She runs out and gets into her car. Before she shuts the door she lets out a deep, loud cry and tears begin to pour down her face. She tries her hardest to pull herself together when she gets home because she can't face her family knowing that she has failed again at love.

She walks in and finds her father laying on the floor with one pill and an empty bottle of prescription pain medicine laying on the kitchen table.

"*Daddy!*" she screams.

She kneels down sobbing and begs her father to please get up. Cheyenne knows she needs to call 911 but can't pull her mind together long enough to go to the phone.

"*Help!*" she screams "Jesus!"

She runs to get her phone out of her purse. After dialing 911 she hurries back to her father's side. She sees him gasping for air and fading away.

"I'm not ready for this," Cheyenne says. "I'm not ready to lose you, Daddy."

Tears roll down her face as the paramedics arrive and try to resuscitate Stanley. The put him on a gurney and rush him to the hospital. Cheyenne rides alongside her dad in a state of turmoil and fear. She has just lost one man in her life and now was about to lose another.

"God, please save my father. This is too much for me to bare."

When the rest of the family arrives in the waiting room, Felicia calls the Elders at church.

"I need all the prayer warriors to join me as we pray for my husband," Felicia repeats over and over again on the phone.

While Cheyenne is happy that her mom is seeking prayer from their church family, a part of her feels like her mom is putting on a show for the whole church just to see her and be concerned for her, not her father. Cheyenne ignores her thoughts and decides to pay her no mind because her concern is all about her daddy.

Patrice is mostly quiet as she rocks back and forth. This is new for her because she always had questions or answers for something or everything.

"Where is Curtis? Shouldn't you call him?" Patrice finally asks.

"I can't. He's dead," Cheyenne replies. Patrice and Felicia stop and look at her. But before they can comment on her response she quickly walks away.

Several days pass and Stanley is growing stronger every day. But he has to stay in the hospital for psychological evaluations.

At home Cheyenne has no one to talk to. Shanice has called all evening, but she just can't talk to anyone, especially not Curtis.

Felicia knocks on Cheyenne's door.

"Come in."

Her mom walks in and sits on Cheyenne's bed where she is laying under the covers. "I want you to know your father and I have been having some serious issues lately, and I think he just doesn't know how to handle it anymore. We have to pray for him."

Felicia grabs her hand and they bow their heads in prayer. "Father, we come to you today as *humble* as we know how. Giving you *all* the glory and *all* the praise. Thank you, Father, for *dying* on the cross. Thank you for *the* blood. The blood you shed for me on Calvary. Lord, you've been so *good*, so good to *me*."

After ten minutes of praying Cheyenne can't help it but notice her mom is talking about herself the whole time and her dad's name hasn't come up once. *Maybe she's forgotten who she's praying for.* But she lets it go—until she can't hold it any longer.

"Mommy, why are you so hard on him?" she asks. "He loves you."

"Because I have some demons I'm dealing with too, Cheyenne. I don't think I have been a good wife and mother, and I blame your dad for everything when nothing has really been his fault. I've tried to make him feel like he is the bad person in this situation, but I have to take responsibility for my own issues. I blamed him for everything that has happened to you. The rape, the molestation, the way you feel about yourself, everything. When the truth is, I'm the one who has not watched over you and given you the love you need. I've been so wrapped up in my career I have forgotten about all that God has blessed me with. My family. I see that now."

"Mommy, you need to be sharing all this with Daddy. I have my own problems," Cheyenne says and rolls over to go to sleep.

Her mother is dumbfounded but takes heed to her daughter's commands, whispering, "She's right," as she turns off the light and exits the room.

Everyone in the family has some things they have to deal with. Her problems can wait.

Cheyenne is standing over the dead body of a man that appears to be Curtis. He's dressed as a prince in shiny armor and groomed to a T. She cries at the passing of her true love.

As he lays there, Cheyenne voices to avenge his death. She'll get even if it's the last thing she does. Once she makes this decision, she looks over and her father is bound by chains. He had been beaten, tormented, and looks like he had not eaten in weeks. Cheyenne cries and cries as she walks into the wilderness. She decides to take a seat because she was exhausted from walking and crying. Before she can get comfortable a small old lady walks past her.

"Why do you weep my child?" she asks.

"My father, the king, is in prison and my husband has died."

"Oh my child, my child. He is not the king," she says "What are you talking about, you foolish lady?" Cheyenne barks towards the innocent woman.

"Trust. Trust," she says, pointing towards the sky. "Trust in the Lord with all thy heart and lean not unto your own understanding."

Chapter 10

Cheyenne spends the whole weekend in her room, ignoring every call, anticipating her father coming home so she can take care of him. She realizes that she only has a few more weeks of school until graduation and can't wait because she will never have to see Curtis' face again as he will be going off to college in the summer.

On Monday morning he comes and knocks on the door. She looks a complete mess.

"I know you know, Cheyenne. Can we talk on the way to school?" Curtis begs.

Cheyenne doesn't want her mother to know she was right about Curtis so she obliges and rides to school with Curtis. Curtis explains that he was going to tell her that he had sex one time with Cydney before they became a couple but just didn't know how to tell her they are going to be having a baby. He was hoping it would just go away.

Cheyenne feels betrayed and suspects he only asked her to be his girl because he needs someone to fall back on for support. He needs to work that out on his own. She doesn't want anything to do with him or his new family and asks that they no longer speak.

He understands and asks if they can still remain friends. Cheyenne doesn't think it's a good idea because it's too painful. She's been hurt all over again before the wounds have healed from Lamar, who's still in jail.

"You said you wouldn't hurt me, Curtis. Now here we are. I thought we would be forever. I had dreams of our wedding, our kids, our big house, and happy family. There's no way I can be your friend. You deal with this. I wish you the best, but I just can't," Cheyenne tells her Prince Charming, the man who made her feel like a queen.

She tries to act like she doesn't care but deep down inside it hurts. It hurts bad. She's distraught over him, not to mention everything that's going on with the man she loves the most. She's trying to hold it all together.

"I'm so sorry, Cheyenne. I don't mean for any of this to happen. I was going to tell you. I swear I was," Curtis says with tears in his eyes.

Cheyenne looks over at him and sees the sincerity in his face, but knows it's way too much to handle. "I don't want to be your friend. This is it." She gets her backpack, opens the door, and slams it shut, heading to campus crying. "So much for happily ever after."

"I messed up. My one true love," Curtis says and punches his steering wheel. "Lord help me."

Chapter 11

School finally ends. Cheyenne got accepted to the college of her dreams. She has a big dream to get a degree in nursing and start a home health care business with Shanice, who is going to the same college. Cheyenne is also excited to get away from the high school drama with Curtis, Cydney, and everyone looking and laughing at her.

Felicia and Stanley are going through counseling with the church therapist and they seem happier. They were proud to see their daughter walk across the stage with her diploma and encourage her to pursue her dreams.

She plans to live at home for two years to save money then will get her own apartment. She also wants to stay home and keep an eye on her little sister, who is starting to get in some trouble hanging with the wrong crowds.

Within two years Cheyenne completes her accelerated degree, gets a good job at the biggest hospital in the city, and is making great money, however she still feels like there is something missing. She works a lot of long hours but is happy living on her own. A woman who is a part of a small women's business group put her in contact with the director of finance at their local bank. Latasha Mason who has garnered award winning success in business development and bank loan approvals, helps her and Shanice with their business. Eighteen months later

Cheyenne has her business plan, her business license, and is networking to get clients.

She works 50 hours a week but still finds time to build her dream business while Shanice chips in to help with the paperwork and administrative duties.

One afternoon, Cheyenne gets that first call from someone who has learned of her company and is requesting her services. She and Shanice take turns caring for the client who suffered from Alzheimer's as they are the most difficult patients. They soon pick up three more clients and check to see if any of the nurses they went to school with want to pick up some extra cash going to clients' homes and taking care of them. Several are happy to get the extra work.

Cheyenne's service does it all, from providing companionship to changing bed pans but she doesn't mind getting a little dirty. She works hard and loves being her own boss. Sooner than later, Cheyenne cuts back her hours at the hospital and is working most of the time at her business. Their first year's revenue is equal to her hospital salary. And she sees the potential to make more money.

She is doing what she loves—helping people—and makes a good living at it. She is so into her career she stops checking in on her family and doesn't date. She wants something of her own that she can be proud of. Her business and career bring her joy. When she does speak to her family, they constantly remind her to put God first in her business and make it to church every Sunday as a reminder that it is God who provides all abundance and fruitful blessings. Cheyenne isn't hearing that. She secretly resents God for allowing all the traumatic things of her past to happen. She believes everything she has accomplished came from her and her alone.

She receives an award for having the fastest growing women-minority owned business in her region and has many articles written about her in the local newspaper. Everyone knows her name. She is living a good life and helping her parents pay for Patrice's college tuition at Old Dominion University, where she's studying to be a psychologist. Cheyenne is proud of her little sister, who made it through high school unharmed and with no babies. She didn't go through any of the heartbreak and terror that Cheyenne endured.

Cheyenne receives an unexpected phone call from Sabrina, a friend back home she used to go to high school with. She was known for having all the juicy gossip from back home. She knew everybody's business.

"Hey girl, how have you been?" Sabrina excitedly asks.

"I've been good. Sabrina, please tell me you are not pregnant again for the fourth time." Cheyenne jokes.

"No, no, no, girl—at least I don't think," she laughs

"Well, what is it?" Cheyenne asks as she looks through some papers on her desk.

"Mr. Curtis is back in town. I saw him the other day and all he wanted to do is to talk about was his princess."

"His daughter?"

"No fool—you! He doesn't even have any kids," Sabrina shares. There is a short pause. "Oh, you don't know?"

"Know what?"

"Miss Hot Pants Cydney lied. That was not his baby. Girl, his mama was not about to let him sign that birth certificate once she saw that baby. Honestly, that baby looked Chinese or something," Sabrina says, bursting into a big laugh. "The DNA test showed that Curtis was not the child's father."

Cheyenne feels relieved. Not for herself but for Curtis. He has such a bright future and is a really nice guy whom she cares a lot for, just as a person. You just can't turn your feelings off for someone who you had such a spiritual connection with.

She reminisces about their chemistry and thinks back to the love and the laughter they shared. He was a good friend. Loyal, reliable, and he was so kind to her.

"So what's he doing in DC?" Cheyenne asks.

"He's doing construction."

"Construction?" Cheyenne is shocked.

"I know, girl. That's what I say. I thought he'd be either playing for the NBA or a Dr. Something by now."

"Yeah, me too."

Something must have happened, she thinks. He is so intelligent and construction was not in his plans. He had dreams bigger than one could even imagine.

"Anyway, my baby daddy is calling me" Sabrina says.

"Which one?" Cheyenne jokes. "Okay, girl. Nice hearing from you and glad to hear you are doing well. Let's do lunch one day soon.".

"Okay. Now go get yo man, girl. Bye!"

Cheyenne hangs up. *Man. Construction. I just can't see that. Maybe he owns the company?* She immediately picks up the phone and calls Shanice despite knowing she's servicing one of their patients.

"Girl, guess what I just heard?"

"What?" Shanice asks.

"Curtis is back in the area and that baby was not his—"

Shanice cuts her off. "Girl, I knew that. I just don't want to bring up that old mess. You had been through so much and seemed so happy," she explains. "Sabrina told me Cydney is living as a single mom in Section 8 housing. The daddy was nowhere to be found and she was left stuck caring for the child all by herself."

Cheyenne has to stop herself because she realizes she is happy at the misfortune of someone else and feels sad for a moment. She hates Cydney for what she did to her relationship but can't imagine what she's going through.

It has to be rough for her.

"Hey," Shanice says, breaking Cheyenne's reverie, "I saw Curtis about a month ago and he asked about you. He read about you all the way in Raleigh and says he came back here to get his woman."

Giggling, Cheyenne asks for clarification.

"He says he came back for you and when the time was right he would be coming to get his princess and sweep her off her feet. He gave up a good job to come and work for his friend's construction company. He says he did it all for you. I have his number. You want it?" Shanice asks her business partner and best friend.

Cheyenne pauses a few moments trying to take in what Shanice just told her. She feels flattered and nervous at the same time.

"No, don't give it to me. If he was serious, he will find me…when the time is right."

"Okay. Bye, girl. I have to go get some groceries for Mrs. Hollingsworth. Her son doesn't do nothing for her."

Cheyenne sets her cell phone down on her custom built, wood-grained desk. She looks around her luxurious office and smiles. *So, he's going to come sweep me off my feet, huh? He came back for me?* She blushes and giggles.

Chapter 12

Cheyenne now has just a little pep in her step as she leaves her office in the evenings. A few weeks after hearing Curtis' name she gets in her car and starts it, but then immediately turns the engine off as she feels something come over her.

"Father, I know it's been awhile since I talked to you, but I miss him. He was my king. He was my everything at one time. I want him back. Please, Father...give me back my king."

Cheyenne isn't thinking about the words she is praying to God. All she knows is that ever since the day she found out Curtis still wants her, his princess, it's all she can think about. Cheyenne wants Curtis and only Curtis. Many guys try to get her attention but she doesn't pay them any attention. It is only Curtis Thompson who holds her heart and she knows that if she prays for it hard enough God will give it to her. In church she learned to pray for God's will.

But what if God doesn't want this for me? she often thinks. But always answers that with: *I don't care, I want him and only him.*

An unidentified number comes up on Cheyenne's cell phone and she quickly answers—she's a business woman and anytime a new number comes up it's either a referral or a new client.

"Hi, this is Cheyenne Hudson."

"You sound just as beautiful as I remember."

"Who is this?" Cheyenne asks, even though she knows exactly who it is.

"Who does it sound like?" Curtis says, his voice much deeper and mature than she remembers.

She laughs like a ten-year-old school girl. "Curtis! What are you doing calling me? How did you get my telephone number? Where are you?" Cheyenne rattles off questions.

"You are a superstar. It's easy to find you. I'm so proud of you, woman!"

"Thank you." Cheyenne blushes.

"I'm back in the area helping a friend get his business off the ground…," Curtis pauses. "Let me stop lying. I came back home for you. I could not stop thinking about you from the moment you slammed my car door. I swear my heart broke that day."

They both laugh.

"Yeah, yeah, yeah," Cheyenne responds like she doesn't believe him.

"The girl lied and the baby was not mine, so I went to Duke and played some ball, but I just wasn't feeling complete," he says. "I kept asking God to send someone like you, but no one even half-way added up. No one was worth my time so I said: *I'm going to go get my girl.* So here I am."

"You think I'm just going to come running into your arms just like that? It's not that easy, Curtis." Cheyenne feels good about herself for saying it.

Curtis is turned on by this new Cheyenne. She sounds surer of herself. He admires it but she must have forgotten who she is speaking to.

"When can I see you? I want to come over. I already know you don't have a man, so you've been waiting on me too," Curtis says. "Ain't none of these dudes like me, and you know it. They can try but baby I'm that dude."

Cheyenne says smiling, "Okay, now that's the Curtis I remember."

They both laugh.

"I'm on my way to the cleaners then to run home for a sec. Let's meet at Angelino's. It's a new Italian place on Richmond Highway," Cheyenne says, feeling like she just spoke to him yesterday even though it's been five years since they last spoke.

"I'm on my way."

"It may take me an hour," Cheyenne warns him.

"I'll wait. I've waited all my life for this," he says.

Cheyenne blushes again. "Okay. Bye-bye."

She starts her car but doesn't put it in drive. She cries out to Jesus and asks that this time it will be right. Even though she has accomplished so much, love is missing in her life. Curtis is her soulmate and he's come back to find her, just like a prince in shining armor.

Chapter 13

"Now you may kiss the bride," says the clergyman.

Cheyenne and Curtis kiss each other softly as though none of the two hundred guests at their wedding are watching intensely. Cheyenne smiles at her groom as her lips part slowly from his.

"Prince Charming," she whispers.

The Thompson wedding looks as if it is straight from a fairy tale. St. Mary's Cathedral supplies just the right lighting to make Cheyenne feel like she and her prince are royalty. The light reflects perfectly off her stark white, hand-beaded gown showing its magnificent grace and beauty, which took four months to create. Rich and full of charm, her long train is the highlight of her wedding dress. She feels absolutely beautiful.

As she stands there gazing at her prince all she can hear in her head is: *This is your happily ever after.*

Rice is thrown as the two lovebirds exit the cathedral into the July heat with bright smiles. They are glowing as they enter their all white limousine. They dance the night away at their handsomely decorated reception. Cheyenne had hired Washington DC's best wedding designer, who had created the wedding reception she always dreamed of. It's stunning and perfect. Cheyenne enjoys sitting just a tad higher than everyone else so her guests have to look up to the newlyweds as royalty.

On the dance floor, Curtis turns Cheyenne around and whispers, "My queen," while admiring how radiant his beautiful bride looks. He knows he's the luckiest man alive. Cheyenne looks in his eyes so deeply, it's as if she's looking into his soul and says, "My king."

Curtis whisks her away to their honeymoon in Waikiki, Hawaii, and they spend two weeks showing each other how true their love is.

But soon the honeymoon is over.

Curtis had promised Cheyenne that he would take care of her and that he preferred that she let him be the man of the house. That meant her no longer working and having dinner cooked for him when he got home from his construction job.

"Shanice, I am going to turn the business over completely to you. Curtis and I are planning to have a baby soon, and he really likes for me to be home," Cheyenne tells her friend. "He doesn't like me working all the time and coming home to an empty house."

"Are you sure? This was *your* dream." Shanice believes her friend is making a big mistake by giving in to Curtis' insecurities. Shanice knows Curtis has a big ego. He doesn't like it that Cheyenne is more successful than him. It shames him in front of his friends and family to take money from his wife, as if it somehow makes him less of a man.

"Yes, I'm sure. The Word says the man is the head of the house," Cheyenne explains. She has a very strong faith and wants to do nothing more than be a good wife and one day a good mother. Curtis treats her like a Queen. She doesn't need anything. He massages and washes her feet when she is tired. He rubs her back and gives her money to go shopping and lets her have the freedom she needs to feel beautiful.

"Okay, Cheyenne, but can I tell you something though?" Shanice asks and does not wait for an answer. "I think you're making a bad decision. But if you're happy, I'm happy for you. Love you and call me when you need me."

"I love you too, Shanice. Thank you for understanding. We'll get all the paperwork handled soon. Larry is well-trained. He's an excellent assistant. He can take over for me."

Shanice can't believe she's giving it all up just like that. She's worked so hard to grow the business and make a name for herself. But she *is* happy for her best friend. She knows that Curtis is Cheyenne's dream guy. Shanice hopes that she'll find someone like him, but in the meantime will tend to her business, go to church, and trust the right one will find her.

After Cheyenne hangs up she cooks her new husband his favorite meal: steak smothered with mushrooms, garlic mashed potatoes, and corn on the cob. She isn't really a wine drinker, but she wanted to add a little something to their special evening.

When Curtis comes home he's very pleased with his wife's set up. She knows how to pick the right pieces to decorate their home and the house smells good, a blend of home-cooking and sweet perfume. Cheyenne is wearing a floor length, see-through lace ensemble and Curtis can't keep his eyes off his beautiful wife. Although he liked her when she was more heavy, he did admire her new body she worked hard to keep firm and in shape. She was all he could think about when he went away to college. She was in his dreams and he even called other women by her name by mistake a few times. Theirs was surely a match made in heaven. Their chemistry is golden and created in heaven.

Before Curtis can finish his meal, his wife's hands are all over him. She wants him so badly. She slowly and gently removes his shirt and kisses his chest, then more forcefully on his neck. She massages his back and shoulders to relax his body.

"That feels so good, Chey," he moans.

She knows it does. She walks over to the stereo and puts on some slow music, promising herself to enjoy a night with her husband that he will always remember.

The next morning Curtis kisses his wife goodbye and for the first time in eight months Cheyenne feels lonely. She has nothing to do. The house is clean. All the clothes are put up. There's gas in the car, her feet and hands are freshly done. She doesn't need any more shoes…so what is she to do? She had gotten use to handling so many moving parts in her life before Curtis came back into her life.

She looks around the house trying to figure out what she can do then just says forget it and plops down on the couch. As soon as she gets comfortable her telephone rings. It's her dad.

"Hey, Cheyenne. I hate to bother you but Patrice needs money to cover her textbooks and mom and I don't have all of it. We had to pay her tuition bill and buy her some groceries," Stanley says.

"Say no more. I'll call her," Cheyenne says.

She immediately hangs up and calls her sister's school to add money to her account. It feels good to do something responsible for someone else other than herself and Curtis.

Cheyenne decides to go volunteer at the church daycare. She trained the caregivers in CPR a few months back and they always love it when she comes and reads to the children.

She arrives feeling alive. She's on cloud nine from knowing she has an incredible man and is able to do something for others. She's such a giver. Cheyenne stays the entire day with the kids. Playing games and pretend sewing with them on the toy sewing machines. She's so tickled because she has no idea how to really sew but isn't going to let them down.

One of the parents come to pick up her son and asks Cheyenne her name, saying she looks familiar. Cheyenne tells her and the petite woman kindly asks her to come outside so she can share something with her.

Cheyenne is a little wary, but agrees because it seems like an urgent matter.

"Your husband is Curtis right?" the woman asks.

"Yes," Cheyenne smiles.

"I'm Ginger, Thomas' wife."

Cheyenne looks puzzled.

"Thomas is Curtis' boss. My husband owns the company he works for," the woman explains.

Cheyenne is taken aback because she realizes she has never met Curtis' boss or any of his friends for that matter. "Oh, okay. Nice to meet you. We should all get together for dinner sometime. I'd love to invite you guys over. Curtis speaks about his job all the time. He loves it!" Cheyenne says.

"Well, I'm only telling you this because I would want to know if it was my husband. I'm going to just say it." She pauses. "Curtis brings other girls by the house after they get off work."

Cheyenne doesn't believe her. "You're crazy. My husband comes straight home from work at 7:00 p.m. every night."

"*Well*, they get off at 2:00 p.m. because Thomas only has part-time hours available now. Things are slow. They come straight to our house with beer and Curtis always has a woman with him."

"Lady, bye. You're full of it."

Cheyenne doesn't want to hear anymore and walks back into the daycare to finish playing with the kids until they are all picked up. As soon as she gets home she feels sick. She runs into the bathroom and throws up her lunch. Her stomach is killing her and she feels dizzy. She and Curtis have been trying to get pregnant for the last few months so she grabs a pregnancy test from under the counter.

She is pregnant.

Cheyenne immediately dismisses every word from that woman who is trying to tear up her happy marriage. There is no way Curtis would do this to her. He came back for her. They are a match made by God. Surely if God brought him back to her, nothing like this would ever happen.

Chapter 14

"Curtis, be sure to come home on time tonight because I made an evening appointment for my five-month checkup so you can come. I want you to meet the doctor, plus you've been coming home later than usual. I never know when to start cooking dinner. Can you please be home by five o'clock today?" Cheyenne begs

"Yeah, sure," he says, kissing her on the forehead.

Five o'clock has come and gone. Cheyenne is so upset she doesn't even go to her doctor's appointment. She doesn't want to show up alone—again. Even though she has a wedding ring on her left finger she still feels odd not having Curtis there, as though people are judging her.

Curtis comes home at 11:00 p.m. intoxicated. He's slurring his words and talking very foul to Cheyenne, demanding she get in the shower because she stinks and that she comb her hair. She doesn't recognize this man who came through the door.

She warms up his plate and places it on the table for him and asks him to come eat. He sits down but only to throw the food on the kitchen floor.

This man has lost his mind. Those are my good plates too, Cheyenne thinks. She asks, "What is wrong with you?"

"Shut yourself up!" Curtis barks. "Don't you *ever* question me!"

Cheyenne goes to calm him down by touching his shoulder but he pushes her away. She walks back to try to console him, this time he gets up and pushes her forcedly against the wall. She's five months pregnant and decides it's best to leave him alone and let his drunken behavior wear off. She goes into their bedroom alone and cried herself to sleep. When she wakes up the next morning Curtis is gone. She calls him and he apologizes, saying he left because he could not face her. He says he's so ashamed of what he did to her and had to get away.

"Get away to where, Curtis?"

"I just came to my boy's house. I grabbed my clothes for work so I will see you later tonight. I'm sorry, baby. It won't happen again."

Cheyenne cleans up the mess he left in the kitchen from the night before and takes his apology to heart. She knows he meant it because he has never before come home drunk and has never, ever put his hands on her.

She grabs her Bible and reads Psalms 91: 1-16:

> *He that dwelleth in the secret place of the most High shall abide under the shadow of the Almighty.*
>
> *I will say of the Lord, He is my refuge and my fortress: my God; in him will I trust.*
>
> *Surely he shall deliver thee from the snare of the fowler, and from the noisome pestilence.*
>
> *He shall cover thee with his feathers, and under his wings shalt thou trust: his truth shall be thy shield and buckler.*

Thou shalt not be afraid for the terror by night; nor for the arrow that flieth by day;

Nor for the pestilence that walketh in darkness; nor for the destruction that wasteth at noonday.

A thousand shall fall at thy side, and ten thousand at thy right hand; but it shall not come nigh thee.

Only with thine eyes shalt thou behold and see the reward of the wicked.

Because thou hast make the Lord, which is my refuge, even the most High, thy habitation;

There shall no evil befall thee, neither shall any plague come nigh thy dwelling.

For he shall give his angels charge over thee, to keep thee in all thy ways.

They shall bear thee up in their hands, lest thou dash thy foot against a stone.

Thou shalt tread upon the lion and adder: the young lion and the dragon shalt thou trample under feet.

Because he hath set his love upon me, therefore will I deliver him: I will set him on high, because he hath known my name.

He shall call upon me, and I will answer him: I will be with him in trouble; I will deliver him, and honor him.

With long life will I satisfy him, and shew him my salvation.

She prays for God to watch over her family and asks Him to make things better when the baby arrives and promises to be a better wife.

When Curtis comes home, she is wearing make-up, dressed up, and her hair was laying pretty down her back.

"Where the hell you been?" Curtis demands.

"Nowhere. I just wanted to look good for you when you came home today," she says. "Don't you miss me looking nice when you come home from a long day from work?"

"You do look good. You just better not be looking good for nobody else," Curtis warns jokingly.

She blushes. "Whatever, boy. You know you are the only one for me. Come eat your dinner."

They have a nice dinner together and everything is back to normal. They laugh and watch TV together the entire week. Curtis comes home on time, cuddles with his wife, and rubs her belly singing to the baby. Everything is great.

Cheyenne's text alert sounds after 10:00 p.m. Curtis watches as she reads the text and smiles.

"Who was that?" he asks.

"My dad."

He abruptly grabs the phone off her lap and nearly knocks her off the couch. He goes through all the messages on her phone.

"Why are you going through my phone? I told you it was my dad."

"*Shut up!* You better not be having no guys' numbers in your phone. That's what I'm looking to see."

Cheyenne does not say anything because even though she's heard about Curtis and his female friends, she never feels the urge to have male friends. She is a good wife and will stand by her man through thick and thin.

Cheyenne reaches over to retrieve her phone so she can text her dad back and Curtis surprises her by throwing it against the wall and breaking it.

She goes and picks up the pieces. "*Why did you do that!*"

"I saw some guy's number in there I don't know. I'd like to see you try and all him now," Curtis says, walking to their bedroom with the strut of a champion.

Cheyenne sits on the floor in shock but is extremely ticked off. She prays and prays for her husband.

Chapter 15

"What's up, Chi? It's Lamar," says a random text message with no name attached to it. Cheyenne reads it in disbelief and immediately gets angry.

Where was he? How did he get her number? What is he doing texting her? All she can think about is, *Oh, my God—what if Curtis finds out he has my number?*

She immediately texts back and tells him to never text her again and that she wants nothing to do with him.

He texts back right away.

> *I just want you to know I'm home and I'm sorry. I have given my life to Christ, and I'm a new man. I got baptized last Wednesday, and I'm filled with his holy spirit. I know there will never be us again, but I had to reach out to let you know that I am a changed man. Prison did me some good.*

Cheyenne texts back and tells him she is proud of him for giving his life to Jesus. Now he can live an abundant life and meet God in Heaven. They text each other for a full hour talking about the love of Jesus and how good He is.

Lamar's last text reads: *Can I see you one last time?*

She doesn't reply and he doesn't text again.

⚜ ⚜ ⚜

Cheyenne and Curtis are eating dinner. She hears her text alert but ignores it. Her phone is on the counter next to Curtis'. A few minutes later, text message alert goes off again. Curtis goes over to her phone and reads the text.

> *Hi, Chi. It's Lamar. You never answered my question. Can I see you one last time?*

Curtis walks over, picks up his eight-month pregnant wife completely off her chair by the neck, and throws her down to the floor. Screaming vile obscenities, he kicks and punches her while she tries to get away from his blows. The next door neighbor's light comes on and he storms out of the house.

Cheyenne is left bleeding and crying.

Chapter 16

Cheyenne has her beautiful baby girl at 3:06 a.m. on August 26 one month before her due date. Curtis is not there, but his mother and sisters are along with her mom, dad, and baby sister. They are all gleaming over baby Maya Thompson. Felicia plans to stay for a month to help her daughter with the baby.

The day Cheyenne gets home from the hospital, Curtis shows up and asks her if he can see his child. Cheyenne agrees but Felicia will not leave them alone.

Curtis smiles at his baby. "She looks just like you: beautiful," he says to Cheyenne. He rocks the baby back to sleep then gives her over to Cheyenne, who is lying in bed. There were complications with the delivery and she had to have an emergency C-section so she is on bed rest for a week.

Curtis looks at his wife and pleads to come home. "I'm the wrong guy to get mad at you for seeing another guy. I haven't been the most faithful husband, so I deserve it. I don't even want to know anything about the situation. The only thing I need to know is if you still love me and forgive me? I have gotten a better job to take care of you and Maya. Thomas couldn't hold on any longer and closed his company. Now I'm working for twice what he was paying me, so I can be here more with you and the baby. I don't want her to grow up without me."

"Curtis, I never cheated on you. I've always been a good wife. Even after all you've put me through."

At that point Felicia walks out to give them privacy.

Cheyenne continues. "I would never do anything to hurt you, but you have hurt me so bad. You could have killed our baby. I can't allow myself to trust you to not do it again."

"Let me prove I have changed. Let me prove it," he begs. "I'll stay at my mom's and come over whenever you need me. If I ever don't come when you need me, or if I harm you in any way, I promise I'll leave you alone and you'll never see my face again. I promise. We have to make this right. I love you, Cheyenne."

The baby cries and he rushes to pick her up from Cheyenne's arms. "Now, now girl, daddy is here. There will be none of that crying. You hungry?"

It just melts Cheyenne's heart and she falls asleep.

Cheyenne is sitting in a rocking chair humming, 'This little light of mine, I'm going to let it shine' while holding her baby. Suddenly the lights go out and it is just her alone with the child in the dark. In the background she can hear Curtis calling for her. He's searching, trying to find his way to them in the dark.

She cries out to him, "Curtis! Curtis! Please save me! I need you!"

As she sits there his voice fades and he seems further and further away. She feels alone. She is alone.

When she wakes up Curtis is gone but her mother is right there by her side.

"Where's Curtis?" Cheyenne asks.

"He went to Linda's. He says call him and he will come whenever you need him. He left his work schedule and supervisor's number."

"Mom, what do you think I should do?"

"Cheyenne, you have to follow your heart. Marriage is forever. It has its ups and downs, but you both have to want to make it work. However, if he puts his hands on my baby again, I'll kill him myself."

Cheyenne decides to give him one more chance. Maya needs her father, but he will have to prove himself. She only wants to be married once, even if taking him back means sacrificing her happiness.

Maya is a month old and Cheyenne is finally walking around better. Her mom is still helping to cook and clean up around the house because Curtis has not been around at all and has not been contributing financially to the family. When Felicia leaves to go home Cheyenne randomly texts Curtis to see how fast he comes over.

He arrives, drunk. Cheyenne asks him to leave and he refuses. She picks up Maya and her keys, intending to leave.

Curtis snatches the keys from her hand. "Where do you think you're going? Sit down." He sweeps his leg under hers, upending her onto the floor while holding their baby. She crawls toward the front door, screaming for help, Maya shrieking in terror. Curtis kicks Cheyenne in the face then runs out of the house, still holding her keys.

She walks herself to the hospital, clutching her baby for dear life the whole way.

Chapter 17

Curtis is furious that he just lost his job and decides to rob the corner convenience store where his friend works the night shift. He will see him and know what's up and hand over the money from the vault. He knew his friend would not identify him to the police and Curtis would give him some of the money for keeping his mouth shut. After that he would return to his wife and baby.

Nervously holding a gun hidden in his pocket, Curtis enters the store. "I want you to put all the money in a plastic bag" he orders his friend as his hands are shaking. "Please don't make me use this gun."

The clerk apprehensively puts the money in a plastic bag as quickly as he can. "You don't have to do this, man," he tells Curtis.

"Yea, I do. This is the only way. I'm broke and I have to take care of my family."

Curtis grabs the bag off the counter but on his way out a tall dark young man coming into the store tries to stop him. Curtis looks the guy in the eyes, pulls out his gun, and shoots the guy in the face.

Then he runs for his life.

Chapter 18

Cheyenne attended Curtis's arraignment to see if he would be let out on bail. Afterward Cheyenne comes to the conclusion that she doesn't want to do this anymore. Something inside of her had felt good when the judge told Curtis's attorney that his client would have to stay in jail because he was a flight risk.

Cheyenne drives herself home and sits on the living room floor. She imagines what her life could be like. She takes herself all the way back to the memory of the young teacher's assistant who violated her and she weeps.

She takes herself back to all the name calling and how all the kids that she wished liked her did not. Instead they teased her until she felt like the dirt on the bottom of her shoes.

She remembers how none of the boys in school asked her out. There weren't any love notes, no secret kisses in the bathroom, and no late night calls with boys who found her interesting enough to ask her for her phone number.

She thinks about how even in her adult life other women ignore her, possibly because she is not a threat to them. She doesn't shop at any of the high-end department stores, and she barely keeps her hair up anymore.

These thoughts also bring tears and she weeps some more. She finally stands up and goes into the bathroom, where she still keeps the tiara she's had since she was a little girl. The pretty silver tiara reminds her of how she felt when she was able to wear her princess dress to school. She felt special and pretty. She felt like she could conquer anything.

She places this small tiara on her head and looks in the mirror. She sees a broken woman who has lost herself. She wipes her tears and says, "God, how could you let this happen to me? I've been so faithful to you, and you allow me to be a single mom with a small child to raise all by myself. I have no one now. How could you?" She throws her tiara across the room.

She slides to the floor and cries for a half hour until she can muster up enough strength to get up and go climb into bed.

Chapter 19

Cheyenne gets Maya off to school. As soon as she walks back into her house she heads straight to the cabinet in the kitchen where Curtis keeps liquor. It's eight in the morning but she is yet again having cognac for breakfast as she looks out the window at the birds playing and feeding.

She pours herself drink after drink until she falls asleep.

"The queen is here! The queen is here!" she hears someone shout, and suddenly she hears celebratory screams and shouts of what felt like acknowledgement of her presence.

Someone grabs her hand. "Come this way, Cheyenne, our beautiful queen."

She hears her name so the shouts are for her, but why? She wasn't anyone to be celebrated.

"We are so delighted that you are here. We have been waiting for you and so has the king," says a small man dressed in a burgundy velour suit.

"Where are you taking me? The king?" She asks this short little man.

"Yes, the king. Your father the king."

Boom. Boom. Boom. Boom. Boom

Cheyenne is awakened by loud pounding on her door. She looks through the peep hole and sees that it is the police. She is thrown when they ask if she knows a man named Lamar Owens.

She refuses to answer anything without a lawyer present and tells the officers to leave her porch.

She sits at her kitchen table with nothing to do. She grabs Curtis's pack of cigarettes and takes some hits. She feels her body loosen up and she pours herself another drink. She drinks two glasses of cognac and smokes three cigarettes. She feels she has nothing to do because she gave it all up to be a good wife as she was raised to be. She wants to live up to the Bible's standards of a good wife but feels defeated and questions if it was really supposed to be this way. If so, she surely is not happy with God and how he wishes things to be.

Cheyenne doesn't know what to do. What she is sure of is that the liquor and cigarettes help ease the pain and sorrow of having to tell her two-year-old daughter that her daddy will be going to prison.

Chapter 20

The man Curtis shot is still on life support so he is only convicted of attempted murder. He is sentenced to twenty years. When he calls Cheyenne from prison or when she goes to visit him, Curtis takes his situation out on her. Cheyenne feels he is acting as if what happened is her fault and that she is the bad person. She stops bringing Maya to see him because of his harshness towards them both. She thinks it's best to give him some time and not put any pressure on him.

Cheyenne hasn't heard from Curtis for eight months. She is finally working and off of government assistance. Embarrassed by her situation, she rarely speaks to Shanice or anyone in her family. Her focus is to get on her feet, take care of her daughter, and drink.

Maya often asks when they are going to see daddy and what time would he'll be calling. She misses her dad and wants to hear his voice. Cheyenne assures her that he will soon, but he never does. Cheyenne wishes that Maya would forget about her daddy.

Shanice has tried desperately to reconnect with Cheyenne while she went through her struggles. She is still running the business they started and has told Cheyenne that she can come back any time. But Cheyenne is too lost in her misery and can't summon the courage to face Shanice. She has also lost her confidence. She doesn't believe that she could run the business like she used to. She doesn't feel smart enough. So she struggles day and night with being alone, soothes her now three-year-old daughter who misses her father, and goes to a job she hates day after day.

She becomes numb to everything and the days blend into one another. She secludes herself from everyone, believing it all for the best.

Cheyenne takes the day off to see Curtis, whose prison is a two-hour drive away. She had promised Maya she would contact him to arrange a visit for Maya to see him.

At the prison she is led to an outside area set up with round picnic tables where visitors can sit with the prisoners they are visiting. Curtis walks toward her looking like a totally different person. His hair has grown out and is pulled back in a ponytail and tells her he has given his life to God. He apologizes for not being there for her and Maya and promises he will be in better communication moving forward.

At the end of the visit Cheyenne hugs, but the embrace feels like it's coming from a stranger. She looks Curtis in the eyes. "You've found someone, haven't you?"

"Yes, I've fallen for someone else."

"Who is she, Curtis?"

"Never mind that. It doesn't matter. I'll do whatever you want me to do with the divorce papers."

His words feel like a knife digging into her heart. "Are you serious? After all we've been through?"

Curtis nods his head in shame. "It's the best thing, Cheyenne. You deserve your king, and I can't be that man in here."

Before walking away, she tells him, "You will have a relationship with Maya. She misses you. Let's be in accord for her, okay?"

"Cool. I can do that." He looks over at another man who has his shirt tied in the back to make it look tight around his stomach. The man has long, permed hair and a girlish figure. Curtis smiles at him. Cheyenne leaves secure in knowing she will be okay without Curtis.

On her drive home she speaks to God and asks what is next for her. Her thoughts are interrupted by a call from Lamar's mother, completely out the blue. She tells Cheyenne that Lamar is the man that Curtis shot on that horrible night.

Stunned, Cheyenne pulls the car over. She doesn't know what to say.

How in the world could that happen?

Chapter 21

"Mommy, did you go see daddy? Is he going to call me? Maya asks as she climbs into Cheyenne's car after school.

"Yes, I went to go see him. He says he's going to call you soon. He says they don't get that much time on the phone, so you will have to be patient. Do you know what patience is?"

"It means to wait."

"That's right. And to wait on when God puts it in your daddy's heart to call you, okay?"

"Okay, Mommy."

It's quiet all the way home as Maya plays with her dolls and Cheyenne wonders if Curtis is now dating men. She's also still in shock to learn that the man he shot was Lamar, who is off life-support but struggling to handle his disability. She feels completely drained and cannot help but wonder was the shooting a coincidence. She pushes aside those thoughts. Her priority is her daughter.

"You want ice cream?" Cheyenne asks Maya.

Maya smiles big. "Yes! Yes!"

"Okay, then that's where we are going."

$$\clubsuit\clubsuit\clubsuit$$

"Let's say our prayer," Cheyenne says after Maya puts on her pajamas.

"God, please, pretty please with a cherry on top have my daddy call me. Tell him that I miss him and just want to talk to him. That's all God. Amen."

"Amen."

"Oh, and God, one more thing: take care of my mommy. Please don't let her drink anymore of that bad stuff and smoke those cigarettes. They are so bad for her, God. Thank you. Amen."

Cheyenne doesn't say a word but knows her daughter is right. She often asks God for those very same things herself. But she goes into the cabinet anyway and pulls out her Jack Daniels and a glass. Her phone rings.

It's her boss. Her puts her on notice that unless her performance improves, they will have to let her go. Cheyenne hangs up, feeling bitter and pressured by her boss. In her mind he constantly picks on her and blames her for everything that goes wrong.

She drinks until she blacks out.

The next morning Cheyenne is so mentally, emotionally, and physically sick from drinking and worry over getting fired that she takes two days off from work. She simply cannot handle any drama or stress from her boss.

Chapter 22

One evening Cheyenne witnesses her supervisor, Richard, stealing medications. His shady actions cause a patient to become severally ill because their meds were not the correct dosage. The head supervisor, Mr. Brennan, announces he will be speaking with all the employees to discover why medication is missing.

Cheyenne is nervous and worried because she knows she has to speak up and tell Mr. Brennan what she witnessed, but she is afraid of being considered a snitch.

Maya wants to watch *Cinderella* and Cheyenne is glad to do something that takes her mind away from her issues. They are sitting on the couch enjoying the movie when out the blue Maya asks, "Mommy, am I a princess?" She then goes on to say that one day she would like to marry a prince and live happily ever after.

After the movie Cheyenne is still thinking about the life of Cinderella and how she once wanted to be a queen one day herself. She once wished she could find her Prince Charming so he could take away all of her problems just like in the movie. Cheyenne believes that every girl grows up wanting a Prince Charming to come and change their world. Cheyenne now knows from personal experience that her life is far from a fairy tale and that fairy tales no longer exist. However, secretly in her mind she is still waiting for Prince Charming to come and save her.

Before going to bed that night Maya asks. "Mommy, where is my daddy?"

"He went away for a while but he will be back one day."

"Do you think he loves me?"

"I know he does honey. Your father loves you more than anything in the whole world. Now come here and give mommy a big hug so we can get some sleep."

"Okay, Mommy, I love you."

Cheyenne kisses her forehead. "I love you more princess."

Once in bed Cheyenne's mind won't allow her to sleep. She had always thought that having a child and being a mother would mean she would never feel alone again but lying there all she feels is alone—in so many ways.

"Father, what do I do? You know my heart, and you know I would never try to purposely hurt someone but ethically I must speak up about what I witnessed. Lord, all I ask is that you speak for me tomorrow. I know that if you brought me to this, you will bring me through it. Lord, I know that you will protect me through it all, I trust you."

Even so, she is still afraid she will lose her job if she turns in her boss. Then how will she take care of Maya? She quickly dismisses those negative thoughts and goes to sleep.

> *She is a beautiful princess wearing a gorgeous platinum ball gown. Diamonds cover her neck and wrist. She holds out her hand and Maya's father quickly grabs it. He's dressed in an all-white tuxedo with platinum shoes. They dance around the ball and he whispers in her ear, "I love you, my queen."*

"I'll love you forever, my king" she replies.

He holds up her hand to spin her around but as she turns the room fades to black and the music stops. She's alone, standing in a hallway full of pictures that carry the memories of her life. She glances to the left and sees her graduation photos, to the right her family. She continues walking and sees that every accomplishment she has ever made—or wants to make in the future—is right there in that hallway. The more she walks the photos start to fade away. When she makes it to the end of the hallway all of her pictures and all of her accomplishments are gone. She looks down and sees she is standing there naked. Everything she loved, everything she cherished has been stripped away and all that remains is a Bible at the end of the hall.

A loud banging on the front door wakes Cheyenne up. She opens the door and Patrice rushes in.

"Why aren't you dressed yet?" her sister asks.

"Patrice, it is 6:00 a.m. I still have thirty minutes left on my alarm clock. I told you to be here at 7:00."

"Well, I wanted breakfast and I saw that you just bought a new box of Lucky Charms so I decided to come early to have breakfast before I started work."

"What work are you doing?" Cheyenne asks skeptically. "You don't have a job, girl."

"Excuse me, girl; watching Maya is a full time job."

"This is true. Okay, just don't be too loud and wake her up. I'm going to get dressed since you already ruined my last 30 minutes."

"Girl, whatever."

After showering Cheyenne stands in front of the mirror and recites what she is going to say to Mr. Brennan. She can feel her anxiety growing until it becomes overwhelming and she vomits. Cheyenne has never been one to speak out, always too afraid of the consequences. She hates that about herself.

Patrice walks into the bathroom eating a bowl of cereal. "So something big must be about to happen."

"Why do you say that?"

"I've known you forever, remember? You always vomit when you get nervous. First day of school, first day of work, every interview you've ever done. You gotta just learn how to chill and go with the flow," Patrice says. "Anyway, you're out of milk...I kind of drank it all."

"Well, just make Maya eggs or something."

"*Noooo*, I'm not cooking, even though I love that girl as if she is mine," Patrice says.

"Then you shouldn't have drunk all of her milk."

"Can't you do it?"

"Patrice, that's the whole point of you being here so I can go to work and you can take care of Maya."

Cheyenne considers her sister very lazy and someone who tries to get everything she possibly can out of people. Now she is just adding to Cheyenne's stress over her meeting at work today.

At the meeting she is forced to meet with Mr. Brennan while Richard is standing in the room. Mr. Brennan is very angry because Cheyenne was one of two staff members on duty that day along with Richard working that hall. Richard claims to not know what happened. Cheyenne stumbles with her words and is nervous as usual. Richard who is sitting there begins talking very quickly and loud because he is afraid that she may place the blame on him. In the black community rule number one is no snitching. However, ethically as a professional she had to put her race aside and do what's right. A patient she worked with for years and cared deeply about was in the hospital fighting for his life.

Cheyenne opens her mouth and tells Mr. Brennan that she would like to speak with him alone. He asks Richard to step out of the room and she tells him that she saw Richard at 3:45 on the day in question.

"He took out three pills from Mr. Becker's medication tray and put them in his left pocket and replaced them with three pills he pulled out of his right pocket that looked very similar to the original but were not the same. I was standing around the corner about to walk in to ask him about Mrs. Phillips blood pressure issues earlier when I witnessed it. Soon after he told me that he would handle the medication rounds for the day because I was so busy with Mrs. Phillips.

"I know I should have spoken up earlier, but I feared for my job. I hope you can understand that I deeply regret not bringing this to your attention earlier but I was very afraid. I have seen in the past how Richard has placed blame on other employees and caused them to get fired and I have a four-year-old daughter to take care of."

Mr. Brennan first thanks Cheyenne for having the courage to open up and tell him this. However, not speaking up earlier has led to Mr. Becker fighting for his life. He tells Cheyenne he has no choice but to fire her for not speaking out earlier. Cheyenne breaks into tears, grabs her things, and walks out.

Cheyenne gets in her car and tells God how hurt she is that He forsake her. She is angry with Him because she prayed and she still lost her job. It will be very hard to find another job as a certified nurse assistant that pays as well. Her rent is due soon and her car needed major repairs. She wasn't good at anything in her mind because she was always afraid to really explore. Her job was her comfort zone. She had been there for five years.

She calls her mother and tells her what's happened. Felicia as usual tells her to pray and that God has something better in store.

"I prayed already and still I lost my job."

Felicia quotes her favorite scripture from Roman 8:28. *"For we know that all things work together for good to them that love God, and them who are called according to his purpose."*

Cheyenne rolls her eyes; if ever there was a quote her mother could wear out that was one of them.

"I'll keep Maya tonight," Felicia tells her. "You are in no state to keep my grandbaby. I'm headed over to your house now. Patrice and Maya will be gone by the time you get back home. God doesn't make mistakes honey. You're a child of the King."

"Okay, Mom. I have to go. Bye." Cheyenne hangs up before her mother can respond.

A child of the King…I sure don't feel like it right now.

On her way home she stops by the local liquor store to get a bottle of Jack Daniels. Cheyenne has tried to cut back on drinking since hearing Maya praying for her. But at the moment she can't cope. While paying she looks around to make sure nobody from her mom's church is there. That's the last thing she needs: to have the whole church talking about how sister Cheyenne was walking out of the liquor store with a brand new bottle of Jack. Just another thing they could talk about behind her back.

Last week the rumor was that her husband left her for cheating on him. Before that it was he left because Maya isn't his.

You know that baby don't look like him...

That's the thing about many black churches: the very ones calling themselves saved and sanctified are also the ones that cause the most damage to people's souls. Cheyenne never spoke out against them and never called them out on the words she heard about herself.

As her grandma use to say: "Let them talk; they gonna talk about you anyway."

She could quote that all day but it still wouldn't change the fact that those words hurt. *If they only knew the truth, if they only knew my truth.*

She goes home to an empty house and starts drinking until she passes out on the sofa.

She is walking through the forest dressed as Snow White. She happily skips through the forest as she whistles her favorite gospel tunes back to back. She comes along a cute, little wooden

cabin in the woods with red shutters and red curtains, secluded from everything. She knocks on the door and it opens. Cheyenne needs to use the bathroom so she walks into the empty house and sees red walls and red carpet.

"What's up with this red thing?"

She goes to the bathroom and embroidered on the towel are the letters MOB.

"I wonder who that is? Anyway let me get out of these folks' house before they kill me."

She opens up the bathroom door and standing there is Lamar and six of his friends. They don't speak; they just stare and corner her into the bathroom. Fear immediately consumes her and she faints...

She wakes up in a room full of mirrors. Cheyenne is forced to look only at herself as she hears her mother's words repeated over and over.

"You're a child of the King, honey; you're a child of the King, honey; you're a child of the King..."

She wakes up covered in her own urine. She laughs.

"I'm a child of the King." Then she takes a sip of her Jack.

Chapter 23

Cheyenne is afraid her car will be repossessed so she hides it around the corner. Every day for six months now she prays for God to save her. She just doesn't understand why she has had to endure so much all these years. She continues to question her faith in God—if He loved her so much why does He allow all of these catastrophes in her life.

Why me?

Cheyenne is walking through a crowd in her princess dress and the people yell and call her trash, Medusa, fat, ugly, dumb...

"You'll never be a queen."

The words keep coming like daggers and with every word Cheyenne feels as if she is being stoned.

Cheyenne wakes up crying because she believes all those words are true. She's never had what she really wanted. She feels God has forgotten about her and she will never succeed in life.

She decides that life is not worth living anymore. She would much rather be dead than face her complicated life any further. She goes into her medicine cabinet and takes fifteen Metformin, a diabetes pill that lowers blood sugars.

Maya walks in as Cheyenne begins to get sleepy. "Mommy, I need you to fix my TV. It won't work."

Cheyenne is barely conscious when she tells her daughter, "You don't need me, no one does."

Maya is confused. "But I do need you, Mommy. You're all I have."

Her daughter's words hit her hard. She realizes she is all Maya has. Cheyenne tells Maya to get the phone and call 911.

Maya struggles to tell the operator what is happening, "I don't know, she's just lying on the ground and she looks sleepy…"

Maya watches her mother pass out.

Chapter 24

She is walking into a ginormous castle made from solid gold. In the throne room sits a man covered in all-white silk and linen clothing.

"My child has come home," he says.

"Am I dead?" Cheyenne asks.

"No my child. I am your father, the king. You have been searching for me all your life but I've been right here with you the whole time. Every tear, every hurtful moment, every heartfelt pain…I was there through it all. I have not forgotten about you. You are my child, and I am the great. I am the author and finisher of your life. I am your king. When you accept me, you accept your place in the kingdom. Do you accept?"

"Yes!" She wakes up saying, "I accept my Birthright."

🐾 🐾 🐾

Cheyenne is working for a temp agency but the money is inconsistent and she's barely making it. She needs help and calls her mother, telling her she needs to talk. Felicia is so happy to hear from her and begs her to bring Maya with her.

Cheyenne visits her mom and explains everything she is going through— all the hurt, pain, and fear and how she feels unworthy of love. She admits she lost her faith in God when she was going through her struggles.

Felicia cuts her off. *"For ye have not received the spirit of bondage again to fear; but ye have received the spirit of adoption, are by we cry, Abba,*

Father. The spirit itself beareth witness with our spirit, that we are the-children of God. And if we are a child of God, then we are his heirs. Romans 8:15 KJV

"That means that we are royalty, honey. That means that we have power."

"*If so be that we suffer with Him, that we may be also glorified together. The sufferings of this present time are not worthy with the glory which shall be revealed in us. For the earnest expectations of the creature waiteth for the manifestation of the sons of God.* Romans 16-19

"Do you understand, baby? You are a child of God, honey. Just trust him."

Cheyenne leaves feeling so much better and vows to stay in better contact with her mom and dad, realizing it was her who pushed them away.

Cheyenne accepts her mother's invitation to move in with her parents. She realized that she will have to give up some things and start over.

There is a condition. "In order to move back in this house under my roof you will have to go to church.' Felicia states.

"But, Mom, every time I see the women from your church and I'm with Maya by myself they ask me: *Where is your husband?* and I can't stand that. They think just because I'm a single mom I am to be shamed. I don't think I want to go there, Mom."

Cheyenne recalls how on last Easter the Pastor seemed to get louder when he prayed over her. Like he was specifically asking Jesus to forgive her sins and her sins only. To Cheyenne, the pastor was insinuating that she was sinful for having a child.

Everything he says goes right back to her and her life., like when he was preaching about keeping families together, not being promiscuous, and the life of unwed mothers. She has even heard that people are saying Maya looks like she's homeless. She doesn't like being the one everyone points at and picks on.

Felicia promises she will talk to her friends at church and ask them to treat her with the same love Jesus would, but Cheyenne convinces her mom that she will find her own church.

❧❧❧

Cheyenne is driving when she sees red, white, and blue lights behind her. She pulls over thinking: *Oh no, what did I do?*

"Ma'am. May I see your license and registration please?" the police officer asks.

"Yes, here you are. What did I do?" Cheyenne asks.

"This car has been reported stolen. Please turn it off, step out, and hand over the keys," he orders.

"Wait, this is *my* car."

"Ma'am, this car is reported stolen. I need you to step out," he says firmly.

Cheyenne grabs her phone and purse and does as he requests. She asks if she can call her dad to come pick her up. When her dad arrives they plead with the officer that they will pay the car note off in the morning, but the officer says it's too late.

Cheyenne tells her dad to forget it; she is okay with them taking the car. She is okay with starting over and that she is a child of God. Stanley smiles, so proud to hear his daughter speak this way, knowing she is turning her faith around.

"Okay, officer. Do we need to sign anything?" Stanley asks.

"Nope. Just call the lender in the morning for the repossession and they will tell you what to do," the tow truck driver tells Stanley.

Cheyenne and her dad walk to his car. Cheyenne watches her car as it is towed. She reflects on how God is taking everything away from her now so He can make room for something new to come into her life. She smiled and says to God, "I'm ready for it God. I trust you."

Cheyenne gets in the car and her dad hugs her. "You have greatness right inside of you. God is taking you through this so he can test your faith."

Chapter 25

After a year of living back home Cheyenne is gaining renewal over her life. She is going to a new church, she's met a really nice guy, and Maya is happy to be surrounded by family.

Her hometown is small and most of the people who grew up there still live there. The guy who has taken interest in Cheyenne sends her flowers at work. He calls every day to check on her and constantly shows his admiration for her. However, Cheyenne interprets his kindness as him just wanting something from her that she is not ready to give. She is not at a place yet where she can give anyone her heart. She is still hurt from her previous relationships and still battles with maintaining Maya's relationship with Curtis, who she is divorcing.

Maya wants her father's attention, but he is inconsistent with his communication. Cheyenne sees the pain it causes her daughter, especially when she sees that all the other girls in her pre-school have daddies in their lives. But bringing another man into the picture is not the solution at this time. So even though she finds him extremely attractive, Cheyenne starts ignoring his calls and texts and the relationship quickly fizzles.

She has rebuilt her friendship with Shanice and they are spending more time together. Cheyenne tells Shanice that Curtis shot Lamar and wonders if it was a coincidence or done on purpose. Shanice agrees that Cheyenne should reach out to Lamar.

❦❦❦

Cheyenne and Lamar start communicating by email. He tells Cheyenne to let Curtis know that he forgives him—even though Lamar was shot in the face and has struggled with recovery.

That prompts Cheyenne to pray and study forgiveness. As she peels back those layers within herself, she is able to forgive Lamar and Curtis. She realizes she is healing old wounds that have held her back from her destiny.

Cheyenne sends an email to Lamar:

I am so thankful that God spared your life. I feel that our pain becomes our purpose in life. For all these years I have battled with pain. Pain from people, stories, and circumstances, but all along if I could have just forgiven the people who hurt me, or forgiven myself for the decisions I made, I probably would be in a totally different place right now.

I thank you for forgiving Curtis. I will let him know that and hopefully it will also change his life like it has done mine. We never know why God places people in our lives, but what I am thankful for is you. For your faithfulness, your deliverance, and your forgiveness.

I feel like this will be my final email because we can't stay in our past. I am moving on with more faith and courage as I take on a new journey. Your faithfulness has inspired me to live out loud and do all the things that I want to do with no fear and no excuses and no regrets.

I thank you for your sincerity and understanding and friendship. I know that God is using you to bring others closer to Him. You have surely done that for me.

God bless you and thank you again for reminding me not to question God as He knows what he is doing, always.

Sincerely,

Cheyenne Thompson

Lamar immediately replies.

It's only a miracle that God spared my life. Now go show the world the Queen that lives inside of you!

Cheyenne picks up the phone and calls Shanice. "Hey, I need you to help me start my foundation for teen girls. I want to encourage them to step into their power and realize that they are queens. I feel like this is the calling God has been directing me all along. It's time I listen."

Shanice is stunned and excited. "I love it! Meet me tomorrow at the office."

Chapter 26

Cheyenne pulls up to the old office she once shared with Shanice and feels the spirit of excitement. She walks in and sees not one single thing has changed in their office. Her wooden desks still sit in the same place, her chair and all her belongings are still there.

"Shanice, why haven't you moved all this stuff?"

"Because I can't do that without permission from my business partner." Shanice says, hugging her friend. She is so excited to see Cheyenne back in her happy place.

Cheyenne sits in her chair and meditates on everything that brought her here. She remembers how powerful and confident she felt when she started her business and wonders what it was that held her back for so long. Why hadn't she called her friend? Why was she so afraid?

She continues to open drawers, go through papers, and inhale the scent of the room. This causes her to reflect more on her journey and get in tune with the Heavenly Father.

"God, thank you," she whispers.

"So are you ready?" Shanice asks, putting on her glasses and grabbing a pen and notepad. She sits down and looks Cheyenne in the eyes. "I am so happy you are back."

Cheyenne smiles and they start planning the announcement for Birthright Accepted, which will assist girls ages 10 to 17 to boost their confidence and empower them to walk purposefully in their God-given talents and birthright. The non-profit organization will assist these girls with positive groups of like-minds to keep them on the right track, tutoring assistance and etiquette classes for grace and charm. As well as offer services for young adult women offering a support system, guidance and empowerment to encourage them to regain their confidence so that they can accept their birthright and operate in their God-given gifts, unapologetically. They put together a business plan, strategizing camps, workshops, events, and fundraising efforts.

When they finish the draft, Shanice says, "I have a surprise for you."

Cheyenne frowns. "I hate surprises. Please, I don't think I can take any more surprises after all I've been through Shanice."

"No, it's actually *really* good news."

Shanice goes to her desk, picks up some folders, and pulls out a financial report. She hands it to Cheyenne. The report shows their home health care business has accumulated more than $450,000 in earnings income over the past five years. Cheyenne's face lights up. She's amazed to see how something that God put in her heart to do has affected so many people's lives and done so well.

"Wow, girl, this is incredible. You did this all by yourself?"

"No, I've always had you in my head telling me what to do: *Be sure to show the patient love and attention. Don't take any shortcuts, ever. Be aware of everything that is happening inside and outside of the business so you stay on top of your game.* You had told me all of this and then some and it has always stuck with me and now people are just referring us left and right. I haven't had to pay a cent on advertising."

"Wow," is all Cheyenne can say.

Shanice then hands Cheyenne a check for $225,000. "It's yours. I promised you that we would always be partners, and if it wasn't for you I would have never had the courage to start my own business, let alone sustain one. I kept this going for you so you could return. This was your dream, and I didn't want to let you down."

Shanice leans over and hugs her lifelong friend. "I missed you so much. It's time we get back on the ball and you continue to live a good life. Forget Lamar and Curtis. That was all in your past. You can't let those bad decisions or what they did to you, or even how they made you feel, hold you back any longer. You deserve so much more." Shanice throws her hands up in the air. "Look at this: you did this!"

"You're right, I do deserve better. Thank you for being that one person who never let me down." Cheyenne states. "I'm fully ready to reclaim my birthright."

Chapter 27

Cheyenne wants to invest the money into Birthright Accepted. She thinks it's best to continue staying with her parents because they are helping her out with Maya and she knows she'll be busy establishing her organization. Plus, she really enjoys the company and fellowship of having family around for both her and Maya.

She is still an emotional wreck and deep down there is still more healing to be done. Her prayer is that helping other girls with their self-esteem will help her regain her own confidence and be a better mother for Maya, who hurts daily from no longer having her father in her life.

She is also working at her health care business again, filling in for one of their employees who is on maternity leave. Cheyenne feels she owes it to Shanice to take over the overnight shift until they find a suitable replacement. But the hours leave Cheyenne exhausted all the time. She has a hard time adjusting to the hours but it's sure was better than the work she did at her last job, so she doesn't complain. She has her goals and wants to stick with them.

Cheyenne walks into the house more tired than she has ever felt.

Maya comes running down the stairs, "Mommy, you're home."

As excited as she is to see her daughter, she can't help but feel burdened because sleep is out of the question.

Before Felicia leaves for work she reminds Cheyenne of her meeting with the pastor at noon. She is really dreading going to see the pastor, especially because she is so tired. Maya is clamoring for food so Cheyenne makes pancakes, which she burns because she is dozing off while cooking. She throws the burnt food in the trash, opens the back door to air out the smoke, and screams in frustration at Maya, who is still crying for her pancakes.

Cheyenne pours a bowl of cereal. "Just eat this, Maya. I'm tired and not cooking more pancakes."

Hurt and angry, Maya eats her cereal in silence. Cheyenne sits on the sofa and yearns for a companion to help with the day-to-day struggles that come with being a single mom. Someone to hold and share her deepest dreams with. Someone with an amazing job who treats her like a queen. Someone to be her partner in life as she pursues her dreams.

She's almost 30 and the thought depresses her a little. She hasn't achieved all the things yet in life that she set out to and no were near it, yet she knows there is so much more out there for her. If only she had a helpmate to help with Maya. Someone to share her deepest darkest desires and secrets…she falls asleep.

The phone rings, startling Cheyenne awake. She answers and it's the pastor calling her to see where she is. While on the phone she looks around for Maya. She momentarily freezes when she sees the back door is wide open then rushes outside and finds

Maya's baby cake doll in the middle of the back yard. She screams her daughter's name.

She realizes she's still holding the phone. "Pastor Kirk, my baby is gone! My baby is gone," she shrieks.

The pastor tells her to call the police and he'll be right over. As soon as she hangs up she runs into the woods behind her house but there is no sign of her daughter. She calls her sister.

"Patrice, is Maya over there? Did you come get her while I was sleep?"

"Of course not. Why, what's happened."

Nearly hysterical, Cheyenne tells her then hangs up and calls the police. When her parents arrive she is sitting numb on the couch, unable to speak or move.

"How could you fall asleep?" Felicia asks accusingly.

"You are such a bad mother," Patrice says in disgust.

Cheyenne is in agony. She has never felt such pain. She stumbles to the bathroom, where she paces in circles, desperately trying to think where her baby could be. She looks at herself in the mirror and is overcome by guilt and self-loathing. She smashes the mirror with her fist, collapses on the floor, and curls into an inconsolable ball on the cold bathroom tile. She prays to God begging him to bring her child back safely, she will never let her out of her sight again. Cheyenne cries out to God, quoting scripture after scripture.

"Help me, O Lord my God! Oh, save me according to Your mercy, that they may know that this is Your hand. That You, Lord, have done it!"

Felicia knocks sharply on the door. "Cheyenne, the police are here. They need to ask you a few questions so they can find my granddaughter."

When Cheyenne doesn't answer, Stanley kicks in the bathroom door. He picks Cheyenne off the floor. Looking her straight in her face he says sternly. "Cheyenne, everything is going to be okay. These men will find Maya. I need you to get yourself together."

He walks her slowly into the living room where the police officers are standing and waiting. She sits calmly on the sofa and one of the policemen sits next to her. They ask detailed questions about what she was doing when Maya went missing. Guilt stabs her heart because she only remembers thinking about the absence of a man and how having one there to support her would make her life easier.

"Young lady, what were you doing when you saw her last? Did you fall asleep?" the officer asks her directly, making Cheyenne feel even guiltier.

Realizing she is in no state to answer any questions, the officers head for the front door, telling Felicia they'll be in touch.

"Be sure she gets some rest," one of them adds.

She nods, just as worried about her daughter's mental state as where her granddaughter could be.

Chapter 28

"Cheyenne, you have to eat girl," Shanice says.

She has been coming over to the Hudsons' home to check on her friend. Three days have passed since Maya disappeared. Cheyenne refuses to eat or do anything. She's become numb to everything but will talk to Shanice and even laugh sometimes as Shanice tries so hard to cheer her up.

All the progress she has made with church and regaining her courage to start the girls' camp is just a dull memory.

The phone rings as Shanice is putting away the food she tried to make Cheyenne eat.

"Hello?…Oh my God, you found her?" Shanice yells with joy.

Cheyenne gets up so fast her chair falls over. She runs to Shanice and clutches her arms. "Where is she?"

Shanice puts a finger up, still on the phone. "Okay, here we come."

They get in the car and race to the hospital. Shanice tells Cheyenne that Stanley doesn't know any information about Maya's well-being, only that she's alive.

They arrive at the hospital and learn Maya is in a coma. Cheyenne runs to her bedside and cries. Her feelings are so mixed. She doesn't know whether to be happy that she was found or be sad that she is in a coma and can't speak. The doctors tell her that there is not much hope for the little girl.

Cheyenne's pastor comes the following day and prays for Maya and shares a long, encouraging conversation with Cheyenne. But when Patrice arrives at the hospital, she starts in on her sister.

"See, you can't even raise a child correctly. Are you crazy, Cheyenne? Look at this poor baby. If you knew you were tired--"

Cheyenne cuts her off mid-sentence. "You have no idea what I have been going through raising a child as a single mom and having to nurture a girl whose father doesn't want anything to do with her. I have worked my behind off to take care of myself and my daughter with little help from anybody. I refused welfare. I refuse to live in shelters. You have no idea, so shut up Patrice. As a matter of fact, please leave before I lose it and smack the living daylight out of you."

Patrice puts her hands up, not wanting to hear it. "I'll be in the waiting room with my husband." She rolls her eyes at Cheyenne and walks out the room.

The pastor sits with Cheyenne and encourages her to go to the King as a child of God. He tells her that as a child of God she can just go to him. God has not given us a spirit of fear but of power, love, and a sound mind.

"You have to have faith and he will bring you through."

Cheyenne's family encourages her to go home because she has been there without a shower or real food for two days. Riding home with her father, she remembers what her Pastor told her about how we get rewarded by praying in our quiet places, so she decides to go into her closet and sit with God. She prays and pours out her whole heart and asks God for forgiveness for not acknowledging that He has all the power.

There were so many times she did not want to ask Him for anything because for a while she lost her faith and did not think she deserved His blessings. She remembers that she needs to acknowledge Him and tell Him how great He is as she sits there in prayer, alone.

She cries and tells God that if he gets Maya out of this situation she will do anything. She will be clean and live in holiness and accept her place.

"Father, I come to you today as your child desperately seeking healing for my child. I know I messed up. I tried so hard to be everything I could, and in my moment of weakness I was unable to protect the most precious gift you have ever given to me. Let her open her eyes and witness your glory first hand. All the glory, all the honor and all the praise goes to you. No one can heal her but you. I thank you in advance. In Jesus's sweet name I pray. Amen."

As she opens her eyes she envisions the Lord in his temple. She envisions God standing over her. She looks up and automatically knows that everything is going to be okay. She has accepted all that she is supposed to be, deciding to reclaim her purpose once and for all. She exits the closet and sees her tiara sitting on the top shelf, she smiles and laughs as she realizes her strength. She reminds herself of her past and that if God could bring her through her past situations, he could bring her through her current situation. The tiara reminds her that this is just a trial and she knows she is going to be okay. She takes a quick shower and sneaks off to the hospital to go pray for her daughter.

"God has already healed you. Thank you, God, for healing my child. I'm speaking it in advance because I know that its already done."

As she is praying and thanking God, people are walking into the room, including her family and Maya opens her eyes. She has been healed. Everyone is praising God.

Chapter 29

Cheyenne is living the life she promised God. She has decided that through the power of God she can do all things as it says in Philippian 4:13.

Every morning Cheyenne wakes up and recites daily affirmations to help get her through the day and she finds great strength in them. These daily affirmations create positive thoughts in her mind and help block out negative talk and self-sabotage. She feels so empowered each morning and has confidence by telling herself who she is, that she can do anything she sets her heart, mind, spirit, and soul to. Anything!

"I am worthy. I am blessed. I am the ebony queen."

Cheyenne reaches out to all her old contacts to help with her business and builds a board for her non-profit organization. Shanice is by her side and things are moving stronger than ever. She is serious about her business, meeting with donors to invest in her endeavors of empowering and changing youths' lives. She has become quite the mentor that a lot of girls in her program admire and seek guidance from.

An incredible thing for Cheyenne is using some of the money Shanice gave her to purchase a brand new home. Maya loves the house and is happy. Their relationship is healthy. Maya is actively involved in the camps for girls and participates in the programs, setting up and making sure everything is all good.

Cheyenne's businesses are growing in leaps and bounds. She is creating the life she wants to live. She is noted as a leadership expert in the local newspaper and national news and just doesn't talk the talk but walks boldly in her walk.

She has fully accepted her beauty and her walk with God and it shows. She finally divorces Curtis and gets herself together. She and her organization Birthright Accepted hosted their inaugural Mother-Daughter Princess Ball which serves as a gala to remind women and girls that they *are* the queens who they aspired to be when they were little girls. This gala shines the light on them and their beauty within where they get dolled up with pretty hair and flawless make up and be the true, divine princesses' who God made them to be, without someone else having to define who they are for them. This is a true ladies night out. A moment to be queens and princesses making memories that will last an entire lifetime. Cheyenne purchases tickets and has dresses donated for all the girls in her camp to come and be apart of the grand affair. She has no idea what she's going to say during her speech. She just asks God to give her the right words to say.

Chapter 30

The crowd applauds as Cheyenne walks up the stairs in her beautiful, custom-made gown. She takes the podium and decides that she no longer wants to hide herself. She graciously takes the microphone off the podium and walks towards the front of the stage. Shanice is stunned but stands up and stares proudly as she sees a new Cheyenne who is ready to make her mark in this world.

"I stand here before you all today as a child of God who once didn't love herself and stood in the shadow of others all her life. I stand here with wounds that have yet to heal fully from hurt I have endured in my life. It's amazing that I can stand here today and be seen as an inspiration to others when just a year ago, I never believed in myself and my abilities to stand in my power. I thought I had to wait to be validated, given permission to stand.

"This ball means a lot to me but this beautiful gown does not define me. I can only define myself. I have grown to accept me and all my flaws. The good, the bad, and the ugly. But I know that the little girl within me has finally blossomed into a woman—a woman with confidence who knows she can do anything she puts her mind to. I want to encourage all of you to never give up on life. Stay true to who God made you to be.

Don't try to fit in and don't let it hurt you when others don't accept you.

"For my ladies, know that you are queens. Wait for no man to save you. You are responsible for saving yourself, but it starts from within. You have to know your strength and listen to that voice inside of you who reminds you. Once you give your life to God, He will give you the power you need to walk in your purpose. Each of us has a queen within us. I thought the queen in me came from the outside, but she was right here inside of me the whole time. You know what I did? I denied her a place in this world. I told her she wasn't worthy, and that she wasn't ready. I thank God that I finally reached down deep into my soul and spirit and allowed the real child of God to shine through or I would not be here today. I thank you and my Board of Directors for making this possible, but what I value most is my accomplishment for fully walking in my gift and accepting my birthright. Thank you."

Everyone gives her a standing ovation. She smiles as she glides off the stage looking more radiant and powerful than she ever has before. As she sits back down at her table Maya says, "Mommy, you look like a princess."

Cheyenne tells her daughter, "Thank you, baby. I am, and so are you. Never wait on anyone to tell you who you are. I want you to already know it so no one can tell you any differently. You got it?

"Yes." Maya smiles at her mom in admiration. "I am an ebony queen, just like my Mama!"